"THEIR TIME IS UP!"

Trekking Through the #MeToo Movement and My Bill Cosby Dilemma

Bettye J Thomas-Gilkey, M.A.

CONTENTS

FOREWORD

This all began "on the night of November 8, 2016, while processing the outcome of the Presidential race. Teresa Shook, a retired attorney in Hawaii, posted these five simple words 'I think we should march,' on a private Facebook group page before she went to bed. By the time she awoke the next morning, 10,000 women heeded her call to action, signing on to march around the country while other women were plotting…"

On January 21, 2017, five million women (and their allies) took to the streets around the world to stand up for their rights. This extraordinary movement had been made possible by an impassioned collective of organizers. In less than three months, they had accomplished the unimaginable: Using activism as alchemy, they transformed one of the most divisive moments in American history – the election of Donald Trump – into an unprecedented movement that was both intergenerational and intersectional, embracing all aspects of its participants' identities. And the 653 marches in the United States and sister marches on all seven continents was only the beginning. A wave of protests and activism followed the march and sustained itself through the first year of the new administration.[1]

Cindi Lelve, former editor-in-chief of *Glamour* and *Self* magazines, described her experience like this: "January 21 felt like a miracle. I boarded a D.C. bound bus with fifty of my friends and colleagues, along with my fourteen-year-old daughter and her friends-it was my birthday, and there was no better party. The highways were crowded with buses crammed full of pink hats, the L'Enfant Plaza Metro station (Washington D.C.) was so

1 Excerpt by Jamia Wilson, writer/activist/executive director and publisher of Feminist Press, from *Together We Rise: Behind the Scenes at the Protest Heard Around the World* by the Women's March Organizers and Condé Nast.

jammed that we spent a good hour underground, chatting and patiently inching our way toward the exit. The woman next to me held a sign that read, "My Husband's Chemo Costs $10,000 a Month"; she explained that she'd never been to a protest before, but that the health-care issue had compelled her to show up. 'And also,' she added, 'the misogyny.' The misogyny was what tied all our interests together, but what was magical about the march was that it made visible the fact that we had so many interests. There were grandmothers and grown men, church groups and unions, indigenous women and Black Lives Matter demonstrators... The Women's March helped us understand. The world would continue to spin forward, but only if we push."

U.S. Congresswoman Maxine Waters was there. She said that when she lined up to speak she "could not believe" what she saw. "I heard there would be 250,000 people present; it was more like a million. It was unlike any march I'd been to before. For one thing, there were the pink (pussycat) hats everywhere. The signs were the most creative that I have ever seen. And the women who had organized the march had included people of all cultures and backgrounds in their leadership and planning."

Waters said that "going in I had been feeling disappointed, even a bit resentful, toward the younger generation. I was under the impression that they thought what we had done for women's rights wasn't important. But seeing the size and passion of the crowd and realizing that the younger women there recognized what we had done and that they were carrying our torch made me realize I'd been completely wrong. And as I left the stage and marched with groups of young women, I saw that they did know the history. Some of them even recognized me and called out my name, and it was thrilling to me to connect with the younger generation. We walked from the stage all the way to the White House and I was in a state of euphoria. It was a wonderful, wonderful experience."

"Congressman Waters has been credited with coining the phrase 'RE-CLAIMING MY TIME' as she repeatedly invoked it when her questions were dodged at a White House Committee Meeting. The Women's March Team would incorporate her words (with her blessing) as an official theme for their Women's Convention held in Detroit in late October, 2017. The goal, to bring thousands of new activists together to tap into the power of women as a force for change. On the eve of the Convention, Women's March Organizers reflected on the impact of the march and how they were moving forward."

I'll be honest. Initially I wasn't moved by the Women's Movement because it was my second time around. I recall back in the sixties when Gloria Steinem led the feminist movement, which coincided with the Black revolution. At the time, I couldn't identify with women issues because Black issues were more profound for me personally. I was a woman, but I was black and my family, black. The plight of the black man and his family needed so much support then and even now. At the time, I was prouder of being black than I was of my gender, which had been compromised early on. But at the end of the day, being black was covertly disenfranchising and more hurting, or so I believed. Besides, I wasn't a feminist per se who went around burning my bra and speaking out against men.

Our men were different, or so I was raised to believe. It was a social and cultural thing. We women were conditioned to stand by our men, who had been systematically emasculated mentally, emotionally, and financially by a cruel and unjust system of Jim Crow, segregation, and blatant racism.

Roxane Gay, author of the New York Times best-seller *Bad Feminist* and professor at Purdue University, said it best: "I had misgivings about the march...like many black women and other women of color...I had complicated feelings about the march, how it began, and how this new-found solidarity was so long in coming. It took something as drastic as the election of a white supremacist to motivate women, *en masse*, to march in such a powerful demonstration of unity and repudiation. Somehow, the mass incarceration of black men, the state-sanctioned murder of black men and women of color, the health care disparities between white women and women of color, and so many other issues were not drastic enough to inspire the kind of outrage seen in the months up to and during the Women's March. That was and is disheartening.

"Fifty-three percent of white women and a staggering 62 percent of white women without college degrees voted for Donald Stump; they were more interested in protecting whiteness than womanhood. Nearly a year after the fact, I remain stunned by these statistics. Perhaps, instead of marching, white women should have had frank conversations with each other about what a vote for Donald Trump truly meant for so many marginalized people..."

Out of that movement, the "Nasty Women" spirit was birthed by Nina Mariah Donovan, a spoken-word artist and student at Middle Tennessee State University.

"I am a nasty woman. I'm not as nasty as a man who looks like he bathes in Cheeto-dust. A man whose words are a disc track to America. Electoral college-sanctioned hate speech contaminating the national anthem. I'm not as nasty as Confederate flags being tattooed across my city. Maybe the South actually is going to rise again. Maybe for some it never really fell. Blacks are still in shackles and graves, just for being black. Slavery has been re-interpreted as the prison system in front of people who see melanin as animal skin. I'm not as nasty as a swastika painted on a pride flag and I didn't know devils could be resurrected but I feel Hitler in these streets. A moustache traded for a toupee. Nazis renamed the Cabinet. Electro Conversion Therapy, the new gas chamber shaming the gay out of America, turning rainbows into suicide notes.

"I am not as nasty as racism, fraud, conflict of interest, homophobia, sexual assault, transphobia, white supremacy, misogyny, ignorance, white privilege. I'm not as nasty as using little girls like Pokémon before their bodies have even developed. I am not as nasty as your own daughter being your favorite sex symbol like your wet dreams fused with your own genes.

"But yeah, I'm a nasty woman – a loud, vulgar, proud woman.

"I am not nasty like the combo of Trump and Pence being served to me in that voting booth.

"I'm not nasty like the fight for wage equality. Scarlett Johansson, why were the female actors paid less than half of what the male actors earned last year? See, even when we do go into higher paying jobs our wages are still cut with blades sharpened by testosterone. Why is the work of a black woman and a Hispanic woman worth only 63 and 54 cents of a white man's privileged daughter? This is not a feminist myth. This is inequality.

"So, we are not here to be debunked. We are here to be respected. We are here to be nasty.

"I am nasty like my bloodstains on my bedsheets. We don't actually choose if and when to have our periods. Believe me, if we could, some of us would. We don't like throwing away our favorite pairs of underpants. Tell me, why are tampons and pads still taxed when Viagra and Rogaine are not? Is your erection really more important than protecting the sacred messy part of my womanhood? Is the bloodstain on my jeans not more embarrassing than the thinning of your hair?

"I know it is hard to look at your own entitlement and privilege. You may be afraid of the truth. I am unafraid to be honest. It may sound petty bringing up a few extra cents. It adds up to the pile of change I have yet to see in my country.

"I can't see. My eyes are too busy praying to my feet hoping you don't mistake eye contact for wanting physical contact. Half my life I have been zipping up my smile hoping you don't think I want to unzip your jeans.

"I am unafraid to be nasty because I am nasty like Susan, Elizabeth, Eleanor, Amelia, Rosa, Gloria, Condoleezza, Sonia, Malala, Michelle, Hillary!

"And our pussies ain't for grabbing. They're for reminding you that our walls are stronger than America's ever will be.

"Our pussies are for our pleasure. They are for birthing new generations of filthy, vulgar, nasty, proud, Christian, Muslim, Buddhist, Sikh, you name it, for new generations of nasty women. So, if you a nasty woman, or you love one who is, let me hear you say, hell yeah."

"…with three times as many attendees in Washington as Trump's Inauguration, the record-breaking global Women's March was so powerful that it defied its organizers' expectations, and the media took note. The pink pussy hat appeared on the cover of Time Magazine, Women's March stories trended on social media, and artists evoked the demonstration in viral imagery like Maine Painter Abigail Gray Swartz's rendering of a Black Rosie the Riveter on the cover of the New Yorker. The Women's March team quickly began to discuss how the leverage the momentum had ignited."

The author further states, "as inauguration day came to an end, Women's March organizers prepared to welcome a spirited assortment of seasoned activists, artists, celebrities, former armchair revolutionaries, and first-time demonstrators to the largest single-day protest in history.

"In the days after the march, commentators mused on the scale and power of the crowds, the signs, the emotion. But the Women's March didn't 'just happen.' A team of organizers – including the four co-chairs, Bob Bland, Tamika Mallory, Carmen Perez, and Linda Sarsour, plus Breanne Butler, Cassady Fendlay, Sarah Sophie Flicker, Janaye Ingram, Mia Ives-Rublee, Paola Mendoza, Ginny Suss, Vanessa Wruble, and many other devoted activists – worked long hours and encountered near-constant hurdles.

"They took cues from freedom fighters from the civil rights movement such as Angela Davis, Dolores Huerta, and Bernice King. They adopted strategies from other movements such as Black Lives Matter, the NoDAPL movement, the DREAMer movement, the disability rights movement, and the anti-gun violence movement to set their own mega-movement into motion. And they worked with male allies like Harry Belafonte, Ted Jackson and Michael Skolnik, while putting-and especially women of color-at the center of their leadership structure."

On that day, "the revolution was televised, tweeted, and live-streamed, but flashed by in what felt like a second. Although the march was one of the biggest mass demonstrations in recorded history, each of us experienced our own limited corner of the bigger picture, and the sum is so much more inspiring, insightful, and instructive than the parts we saw in our own individual cities and on our feeds – which is why a deep, behind-the-scenes look is critical to our understanding of what really happened...."

"For several weeks now, the media has been publishing one testimony after another regarding sexual harassment allegations from women against their male perpetrators. Numerous men have been fired, newscasters, actors, politicians and congressmen. Let's not forget that our nation's president opened the door for these behaviors with his cavalier attitude about women and his encouragement to 'grab them by their…[genitals],' speaking of women. He's also gone on record, denigrating women who have less than voluptuous breasts, as well. So, the climate was set by our nation's leaders. It stands to reason that it's been having national and international implications.

"However, women are standing up and speaking out in rebellion. This deluge began with the hashtag story that appeared on Facebook where victim after victim replied '#MeToo' meaning they too had been sexually violated in some manner by a man. The results were startling. Women who appeared to be so strong and successful reported incidents of sexual harassment. Some went into detail…"

Personally, the last straw for me occurred when the handsome and debonair CBS news anchor Matt Lauer was fired from the network for repeated comments/actions over the years that included gifting a woman with a sex toy and attaching a note regarding what he wanted done with that toy!

Then, after reading that a long-standing and prolific Congressman whom I've held in the highest regard for decades and whom I've met personally, U.S. Congressman John Conyers D-Detroit, MI, participated in the same kind of vile behavior, I was saddened, disappointed, and repulsed to the point of recalling my own personal story that kept gnawing at me to be told. I was almost late for work as I stood in front of the early-morning television show, listening to the victim's heartfelt expression of how Conyers "disrobed to his underwear in front of her and requested sexual favors."

I believe it was this gut-wrenching revelation that evoked such strong emotions within me to tell my own story and write this book. I immediately rushed to my computer, typing in haste to share my personal lamentations so that I could finally release the weighty, stinking baggage that had crippled me for so many decades during the debilitating journey.

As Conyers's victim spoke, her pain and shame pierced my own. I believe appearing on live television was the last thing she wanted, but the need to relinquish that soul-breaking baggage far outweighed her fear of reprisal, ridicule, or embarrassment that might possibly ensue. The need to free her mind, literally so her "ass could follow," took precedence over everything else, I do believe.

As I put on my coat and walked out the door, I wondered if the two managers that I worked for in my early twenties ever recalled our passionate trysts during these historic moments of self-disclosure in the wake of #MeToo…for, early in my professional career, I was a young and dumb twenty-three-year-old victim who just wanted to keep my job, failing to realize it would not be the end of the world if I lost it. But the episodes have remained active within my consciousness some forty years later, as if they happened yesterday. The memories don't go away; we merely silence them into our consciousness as "sleeping dogs" we should "let lie," but eventually they begin to BARK LOUDLY!

Many of the so-called preachers and community activists who took me "there" are dead. I'm believing they carried our encounters to the grave. Perhaps they made their peace with God or, feeling entitled to approach women however they saw fit, possibly didn't give them a second thought. But I'm not dead. I'm very much alive and my memory is haunted by numerous long-standing and repeated memories about them.

But those who remain, though they are senior citizens now, know what they did, and so will you when I'm finished writing about it. No need to continue carrying those bags. I'm seeking peace and freedom as I settle into my own winter season. I'm weary now and tired of carrying that baggage. No more "bag lady" for me!

Yes siree!!! I'm about to stick my finger down my literary throat and release these toxins that have been plaguing me for decades. You guys can have it back! Do with it what you will, but keep it away from me!

Hopefully and prayerfully, these short stories will emancipate some- one else who's been on a similar journey and make their life just a tad bit easier, from "faith to faith" and "glory to glory!"

If I knew then what I know now, I'd be a wealthy woman, because I would have prosecuted them. But during those times, women were en- couraged to be quiet and take it to the grave. To that, I can finally exclaim, NO MORE! Besides…my remains will be cremated—all the more urgency for setting the record straight.

The issue of sexual assault is equally as repressive as the homophobia that pressures gays to remain in the closet, forced to live on the down-low, shrouding their hidden desires and lifestyles in secrecy. It's no different! I'm coming out of the closet with mine.

So look out, fellas!!! If you 've been wondering whether I would ever tell, guess what??!! I am! YOUR TIME IS UP! Here it is, my dear!

CHAPTER ONE

The "#MeToo" Movement

Several months ago, I signed on to my Facebook page and saw a deluge of #MeToo comments. I had no idea what it meant until I delved deeper, and then I recalled that I needed to acknowledge my #MeToo as well.

This tip-of-the-iceberg movement all started with journalist Sandra Muller, who "turned to Twitter to recall a humiliating and inappropriate sexual come-on from a powerful French executive." In quoting his lewd comments about her anatomy, she popularized the #BalanceTonPorc—"Expose Your Pig"—movement.

As a result, tens of thousands of Frenchwomen responded to her call and began posting "disturbing accounts of sexual harassment and abuse, although most stopped short of identifying their harassers," according to the *New York Times*.

The scandal surrounding Hollywood producer Harvey Weinstein coincided with Muller's movement, thereby creating an outpour in the United States and elsewhere under the #MeToo cooperative that was also inspired by actress Alyssa Milano.

What's significant about this groundswell of outpouring, however, is the potential impact it may have in propelling much-needed changes in the French culture, which has "long enabled powerful men to misbehave with impunity," both socially and legally. "Legislation is currently underway to fine men for catcalling or lecherous behavior toward women in public, to extend the statute of limitations in cases of sexual assault involving minors and to create a new age ceiling under which minors cannot legally consent to sexual relationships." So much for older men dating teenaged girls…a pedophile by any other name, in my opinion.

As I reflect upon the painful and heart-wrenching Facebook accounts I read from the plethora of "#MeToo" posts, I see that the assaults did not discriminate. There were female judges, lawyers, doctors, churchwomen, and victims from all walks of life whom I could never have imagined enduring the same degree of sexual harassment/assault that I have personally endured. Then there were those who have shared their intimate stories of sexual violence with me that didn't post at all. I found that equally troubling, as it signaled a far greater pain that even a social-media screen could not hide. Yet they still suffer in silence.

Marlène Schiappa, a feminist writer who is France's Secretary of Equality, said, "[W]e all have stories of harassment and assault. One of my best friends said something with the hashtag that she had never told our group of friends. This hashtag movement, with the barrier created by a screen, can help people speak out..."

Although critics argue that "sexual harassment accusations would be better handled in the courtroom than on social media," Ms. Muller, the journalist who initially tweeted the "Expose Your Pig" hashtag, indicated she was overwhelmed by the hundreds of reactions she had received. Meanwhile, two lawyers for the executive she implicated demanded that she delete the tweet. One such lawyer went as far as calling her accusation a "case for defamation," but refused to comment further. Nor did he respond to requests to be interviewed.

This issue of sexual violence against women worldwide is ageless. Whatever it is that makes men believe they can say or do anything to us without retribution must cease. On the other hand, they will accuse us of being anti-male because we demand to be respected and have begun to speak out. It is time for them to realize that we are not here for their jollies or repressed sexual frustrations.

When women speak for ourselves, we are accused of being feminist or women's liberationists. Although there are similarities in the movements, this issue addresses the historical disrespect and disregard that has crippled the psyches and overall self-esteem of women since the beginning of time.

Having a national leader who publicly and proudly condones the practice of "grabbing women" by their private parts without public outcry is reprehensible and fuels the fire for gender inequity and insensitivity in America and throughout the world.

Of equal concern is the administration's attack on women's health via a coalition of senators, representatives, state parties, and national organizations who "are building momentum to deny access to birth control rights for women," according to U.S. Senator Debbie Stabenow (D-MI). In this movement, they are attempting to "roll back the ability to afford birth control because insurance companies won't commit to providing coverage," she said. "As a result, hundreds of thousands of women could lose the birth control that they depend upon."

Meanwhile, women are speaking out with voices that say, "We are mad as heck and not taking any more!" We are far greater than our body parts and it's about time we stood up to be counted.

#METOO!!! "EXPOSE YOUR PIG!"

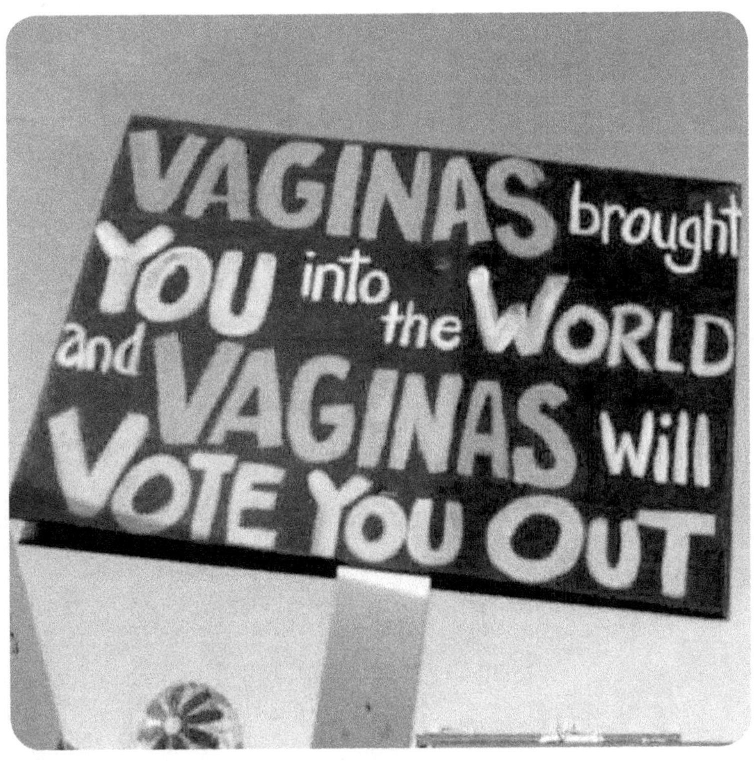

CHAPTER TWO

Groomed for Sexual Assault

I FELT MY DADDY'S ERECTION! YUCKYYYYY! Have you ever felt yours?! A young daughter of any age should not know what her father's erection feels or looks like in any form, at any time!

Mama had sent me into their bedroom to wake Daddy up from another drunken stupor that pulled him into deep sleep before going to work the night shift at the Kellogg Company. It usually hadn't been difficult to awaken him, but as the progression of the disease slowly engulfed him, it was becoming an arduous task. We all had become victims of the bottle. I was twelve years old with an astute awareness based upon my obsession with researching what was happening to my daddy, to our family.

Initially, I shook his foot. Experience had taught me to maintain distance from his wandering hands when he was in this state. Daddy was unresponsive. I shook harder, but still nothing. I could smell the reek of old, cheap vodka seeping from his pores, especially his rotten feet. So I tugged at his leg, which I later learned was not the best place to touch on an inebriated man. How could I know? He stirred but not enough to fully awaken. By the time I reached his shoulders for another shake, Daddy was waking up in ALL his parts. That was when he grabbed me hard and tried to pull me atop him, but feeling his maleness empowered me with a divine strength to push away and run from the room. It's a memory that has NEVER left me.

When I told Mama, who was in the kitchen preparing his lunch, she quietly stopped what she was doing and walked to their bedroom. I ran into mine, which was right next door, and sat on the bed, listening. I NEEDED to hear her protect me, as she had not done before regarding "Daddy."

"WILLIAM! GET YOUR DRUNK ASS UP!" she yelled. "IT'S TIME

TO GO TO WORK! KEEP ON AND GET FIRED, YA HEAR? THEY'RE NOT GOING TO KEEP GIVING YOU CHANCES TO KEEP YOUR DAMN JOB!" And that was it. He got up and she went back to the kitchen. Just. Like. THAT!

My daddy was a pedophile. Mama knew it. The whole family knew it, too. He was also an alcoholic womanizer who I believe was sexually assaulted as a young boy. What can I say? That I knew what sexual assault felt like before I even knew I had feelings? That I was born to be abused? How about this…I was exposed to sexuality probably before I could even walk or talk!

He'd started molesting Louise, my mother's first cousin, when she was ten. Daddy was twenty-six and married to Mama, who took Louise under her wing as a young child and brought her to Michigan when they migrated there in the 1950s. She wanted to give Louise a better life, even though the family warned Mama that she was just like her promiscuous mother. However, her blind love for both betrayers deafened her ears and blinded her eyes to their accusations.

It took twenty-four years for Mama to finally get her fill, when she ran Louise out of town with threats of murder before sunset. I was sixteen years old but vividly recall that near-tragic day.

I don't have proof that I was molested in infancy, but I do recall images that flashed across my mind when our daughter reached the age that I'd been when I was adopted into the Thomas family. Shyann was nine months old. What else could explain the brief but clear picture of my father licking my vagina as I watched my husband change Shyann's diaper? Where would such a vile vision come from?

Apparently, it was so upsetting that the vibe touched Bo, my husband, causing him to look up and see such disdain in my face that he quietly but sadly said, "Don't even think about it, Bettye! I'm not William and you know I would never do anything like that to Shyann. You really need to get help about that, because it's starting to affect you and us!"

He was right. And I did. That year of slaying the sexual-abuse demon took its toll on me and on our family. It was so very intense that I'd come home from weekly sessions so drained that I could barely muster enough energy to drag myself in the door and fall into bed. The therapy went on for several months as I withdrew deeper into myself, often oblivious to my husband and children.

The psychologist was aggressive, thorough, and far-reaching. But I'll tell you what…the dreams about my father sexing me stopped. The secret, sexual images of Daddy that I shared with no one but that periodically popped into my dreams finally ceased to exist. Unfortunately, my family was the sacrifice that I subconsciously made to exorcise the toxic baggage. So much of the damage was irreversible. I tried desperately to save what I could. Bo left me, but poor Michael and Shyann were stuck. Life for them was not a crystal stair.

Nobody knew about the childhood sexual fantasies I'd held about Captain Kangaroo, wondering how big his penis was. Or about the little boys that I played "show me yours and I'll show mine" with behind the garage. Or about how Barbie and Ken ALWAYS took their clothes off to "do it." I could never reveal or understand how I began masturbating when I was barely out of kindergarten. All I knew was that I had this itch deep inside that needed to be scratched. But I did have sense enough to know it wasn't natural for a little girl to feel that way and with that knowledge, I kept those thoughts/feelings captive in my young, easily aroused mind.

When I was around the age of ten, however, Daddy started fondling my budding breasts. It felt good and I felt guilty about it. At the same time, however, I shoved his hands away and avoided him, especially when I realized that he was drunk. I hated the smell of his cheap whiskey breath and the feelings associated with it. He didn't behave that way when he was sober. Eventually, when I could recognize that I had two daddies in one, I started folding my arms across my chest to protect the young twins from his cunning hands.

He got so audacious as to tell Mama that I "never let him hug me anymore!" She in turn had the nerve to question me about it. When I told her what was happening, she accused me of lying. But she knew. Mama knew the man she was married to. She knew how Louise sneaked around with Daddy and how her sisters ran away, laughing nervously, when Daddy came around and "wanted a hug." I remember watching them scurry about and wondered why they behaved that way, but soon understood. Yep. That really happened. #MeToo!

Although I remained a virgin until I was fifteen years old, there was plenty of necking and petting going on. I had this itch, you see… And I liked the big boys. Didn't want anything to do with boys my own age. Mama taught me that one. She said it was "better to be an old man's sweetheart than a young man's fool!" That's right. My mama taught me that. #MeToo.

On my sixteenth birthday, after my parents presented me with the sterling-silver charm bracelet that I still have, my father gave me a secret gift. It was a book. The title of that book was *The Sensuous Man* by "M," and it taught ways to improve lovemaking. This book was the counterpart of *The Sensuous Woman* by "J." In my opinion, the contents were so suggestive that the authors didn't want their full names associated with the sexually explicit material. I guess this was his way of talking to me about the birds and the bees. I sure read it and learned MUCH! That's for sure.

When I lost my virginity during the summer of 1969, I had two young men to choose from. Eeny-meeny-miny-moe. Yes, I said men. Both young men were twenty-one-year-old college students. I had become an older man's sweetheart, just like Mama told me. The guys thought I was sixteen years old. Technically I was still jailbait, but I chose the wrong one to share my gift with. It would be my first round of bad choices in men.

In most black, grassroots communities, it was no biggie for young teens to date grown young men. Girls in their late to mid-teens were prime choices for young men to date and dine, with the sole intent of bedding: a skewed tradition gone awry. Back in the day, the young men married the young virgin and made an honest woman of her. Looking back, I see it as another form of pedophilia. Grown men with teenagers dates back to Biblical times, actually.

Once I got broken in, though, I was "a doozie," as Mama used to say.

She taught me to "always have a spare tire in case one went flat." I took her advice to heart. Then she ridiculed me because of it. I thought she was just jealous, especially when she said I "was acting like a dog in heat." I was a doozie and I was acting like a dog in heat! Promiscuous was the operative word. Saying I was a "doozie" was demonstrative of my mother's diplomacy. One of her many gifts…

Then I met Karl. He was twenty-seven and I was seventeen. Again, pedophilia. If you read *The White Purse* you know what happened in that controlling and abusive relationship. But I was vulnerable, a likely target. Right? He saw me coming and cast the net. Karl turned me out. That "itch" made me stay despite physical and emotional abuse. I was accustomed to the latter, thanks to Mama and Daddy.

In just a few years, my mama, the city's numbers woman, began luring all the big money men to her beautiful, young daughter, and if Mama gave the nod, it was okay, right? Nope. My Aunt Mable and Brotha chastised her for guiding her only daughter in that direction. Of course, she put it on me; free will, she called it. Eventually, between my job as executive secretary and proceeds from my sugar daddy, I made enough money to leave town.

Mama's influence was the driving force behind my relocation to Lansing, Michigan. I had to get away from her, my past, and the influence of Battle Creek. I wanted a new life and needed it just as badly.

Around that time, I began coming into my own, developing a semblance of self-esteem, and wanted to see what it felt like to be "a young man's fool." I wanted to love and be loved in the purest sense. I found that with Michael, but was so terribly damaged by a horrible paradox. He was a good young man and I wasn't his fool, but I was damaged, and he caught HELL dealing with me. But our love was beautiful and pure. He should have been my husband…

So yes, I was groomed for sexual assault.

CHAPTER THREE

Who Is This Weinstein?

"As we get our bearings in this new post Weinstein age, a lot of women have spent their time returning to experiences like this one – holding them up to the light, considering what we might have missed. The difference between that night and many of the stories being reported these days is obvious, and leaps out quickly. It's the similarities that are trickier."

"The most arresting thing about Harvey Weinstein for me, was how methodical he was, how consistent in modus operandi, when he decided to go after a woman: the call from a talent agent to arrange the meeting, the reassuring female assistant in the lobby, the hotel room door closing, the bathrobe, the incongruous request for a massage. There was a ritual sameness to these stories; one that said to us: This was a result of consideration and planning, of practice."

"This treatment of the hunt like a craft, the carefulness of it, is one mark of what, we often call a predator. People like that word because of its certainty, the way it rules on the case all by itself. A predator naturally lives outside the herd, and because of that, he can be very easy to ostracize. The shaming, the firing, the possible criminal prosecution; All of that seems a logical consequence for predators."

"Now the word comes up everywhere, and many of the cases are easy: Weinstein: Roy Moore reportedly chasing teenagers around an Alabama mall, Russell Simmons accused to taking women up to the penthouses and keeping them there against their will. But then there are the other instances – when the behavior is unquestionably wrong and invasive, the consequences are justified and yet the word 'predator' doesn't quite comfortably apply. There are all sorts of men who do all sorts of thing they should not be doing, but who believe themselves exempt from this moment because, well, they're not THAT bad."

"In ecology, a predator is an animal that kills and eats other animals, and the threat it poses is relatively clear cut. There is very little ambiguity when the mountain lion eviscerates the rabbit, or the leopard rips apart the gazelle. But when people talk about human predators, they're looking at them from the standpoint of the gazelle."

"The rhetoric of the predator has been wrapped up for so long with a brutal reading of human nature – a Darwinian vision of hunter and game and cold, remorseless victimization. But what about those who harm other people carelessly, thoughtlessly, drunkenly, ignorant of the consequences. In life, these people seem harder to avoid than the evil ones. They are a strange reminder that words like 'predatory' were used to classify animals. The Latin root of "predator" is not, as you might assume, the word for "hunt" is venari. It's praetor – to plunder. Which is to say, to take what you have already conquered, by right, like a pirate taking a ship's treasure." By Michelle Dean, The New York Times Magazine 12/24/17.

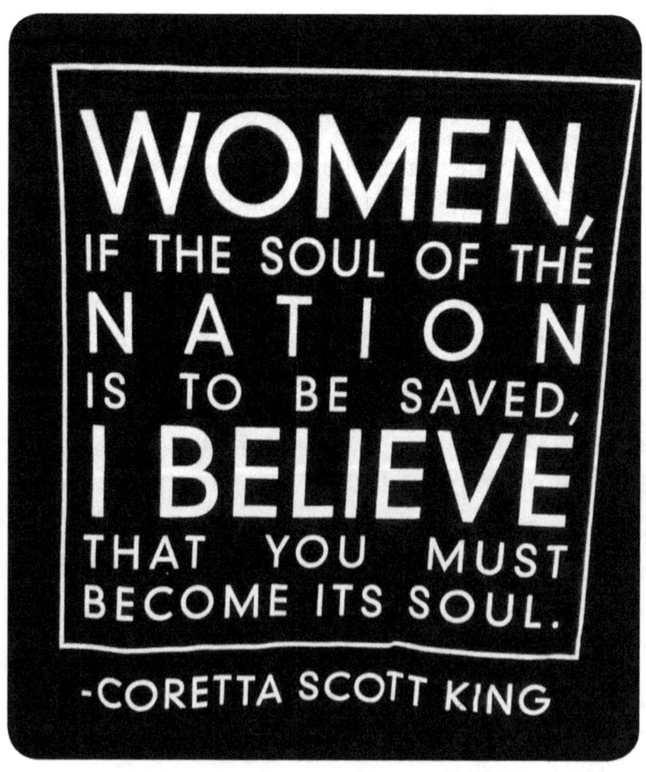

CHAPTER FOUR

"Bettye Has a GOOD JOB!"

When I met him, I had recently graduated from Kellogg Community College (K.C.C.) with my associate degree in legal secretarial studies. My dream was to work for an attorney, but employers in the legal profession wanted someone with experience. Somewhat disappointed, I began working for Manpower, which was a Title IX program that served as a temporary employment agency. It was in a local governmental office building where my chances of being hand-picked from the secretarial pool were great.

Since I was fresh out of college and it was my first professional, high-profile career opportunity after leaving K.C.C.'s Placement Office as a student assistant, I felt accomplished and ready to take the world by storm. I'd ascended from my family's humble beginnings as field workers picking cotton, sharecroppers, "the Help" for private homes, managers at Te-Khi Truck Stop, and workers in Kellogg's factory.

After leaving my job as a private-duty housekeeper and dinner cook at the Te-Khi, I tried a brief stint working at Eaton Corporation in Marshall, Michigan, as a factory worker while I completed my degree at K.C.C. I was raised to believe that I wasn't too good for any kind of work that would make an honest living. So my work ethic was intact and for that I was very proud.

I often ran into Mr. Brown in the hallway where the Manpower office was housed in the impressive, five-story edifice that greatly enhanced my self-esteem and kept me feeling valuable every day I came to work. I was enamored with all the workers who dressed so finely and professionally. The job was a far cry from any I'd ever had.

He always smiled and spoke as he walked quickly like he was going someplace important. I felt honored that he even acknowledged me and always replied in kind. Mr. Brown was the highest-ranking black professional in the building, but he appeared to be such a down-to-earth and personable manager. If I had a choice, I had hopes of working for him one day.

I was in the secretarial pool for two months before I was called into the Manpower director's office. Mr. Brown was sitting there and informed me that he needed a secretary. He asked if I was interested. Initially I was speechless, but I quickly gained my composure and answered "yes" with wide-eyed innocence before asking what the requirements of the position were. The director granted his approval for me to interview and within a week, I was hired to become Mr. Brown's executive secretary.

I had my own desk and sizeable office area that was located right in front of his much larger enclosed office. Our office area was isolated from the rest of our staff of ten people, which made me feel very privileged. A portion of my workload included processing legal documents, so because of my training in college, it was not foreign to me.

The first few months were glorious. I was learning the job, meeting important, high-profile people, and getting exposed to a new professional arena. I loved my job and felt so proud as my parents boasted of "Bettye's big, important job."

Although I wasn't new to the workforce, I was naïve about the nature and politics of the office environment. The nuances and dynamics of working for such a high-profile political figure were quite complex. I was starry-eyed.

But then one day, it happened. Mr. Brown, who many thought to be handsome, came in from lunch and asked me into his office. This was not unusual because I frequented his office throughout the day for messages, briefings, and other job-related tasks. This time was different, though, and I felt it shortly after closing the door. He didn't sit down as usual but was leaning against the front of his desk, right in front of the chair I always sat in. This change of position gave me pause, so I remained standing toward the back of the room beside the door. I could smell alcohol from a distance, which evoked vivid, painful memories of my frisky alcoholic father.

My fight-or-flight instinct launched immediately.

"Why are you standing back there? I'm not going to bite you!" he replied, beckoning me to sit with a strange, sinister smile. "Come here. I can't talk to you from way over there."

As I edged closer, so did he. I was taking baby steps to what I perceived to be his giant leaps. I wanted to run and felt hot tears well inside my eyes because I didn't know how to handle the inevitable. Suddenly, Mr. Brown was in my face and grabbed me hard, pulled me close, and planted a long, sloppy kiss on my trembling lips.

I stood there motionless, afraid of what to do next. But I kept my gaze affixed to the floor. I felt dirty and ashamed, wanting desperately to wipe the slobber off, but my hands wouldn't move. My feet, weighing like concrete blocks, would not move either; otherwise I would have run far, far away. But my queasy, nauseous stomach mobilized me, so I was able to turn around and run into his private bathroom just in time to heave. I was so disappointed in him and in myself for letting it happen. But I didn't want to say anything because I liked my job and didn't want to lose it.

After I flushed the toilet, rinsed my mouth and turned towards the door where my desk was safely awaiting me on the other side, he came toward me and placed his hands on the door, so I couldn't open it. I felt trapped and just wanted him to move. But he wouldn't!

"That bad, huh?" he joked nervously. "Where ya going?" he asked, flashing a smile that was now apprehensive.

"Did you think you could just keep teasing me every day, coming in here looking and smelling so good? You can't be surprised at what just happened!!! Why have you been teasing me like that??"

"TEASING YOU?!" I screeched in a loud whisper. "What are you talking about, Mr. Brown?!"

The look of fear and repulsion upon my face must have said it all. He had crossed the line, and even though I was only twenty-one years old, I had enough sense to understand that my job was now in jeopardy and I stood at his mercy, saddened by the reality of our unstable future together.

My family was so proud of me being HIS executive secretary, but nobody had prepared me for the price I'd have to pay to keep the job.

No, he didn't! Was he trying to blame ME for his actions?! I didn't make him do anything. That was his own weakness and unprofessionalism, and he knew that! I must have glared at him, because this is what he said next.

"Oh. Okay. You're a DICK-teaser, aren't you? That's all right. I won't touch you again. You can leave now," he said abruptly as he turned around to sit high and mighty behind his huge mahogany desk. Immediately, he picked up the phone to make a call, which was his way of saying there was no more discussion. I stood there, motionless. When he saw I wasn't going anywhere, Mr. Brown hung up the phone, looking pitiful.

"I'm sorry," he apologized, as if it was something he had to do. "That wasn't supposed to happen. It won't happen again. You can go back to your desk now."

I walked out of his office feeling dejected, violated, and very confused. I tried to wrap my mind around what had just happened and instead of sitting at my desk, I walked out of the office door into the lobby and took a long walk around the building, ruminating over it all. In retrospect, I believe he knew about sexual harassment, but I didn't. I was young and dumb.

What made it worse was that Karl was jealous and suspicious about Mr. Brown from the onset. Many nights we argued about the late nights I worked during campaign season. The more I worked after-hours, the angrier he became. But I didn't take his accusations seriously because it was his insecure nature to respond that way regarding any man. I wanted to tell him what had happened at work, but couldn't trust his volatile nature. I told Mama instead.

That was when I first head the cliché about "dipping your pen in the company ink" and "eating where you wipe your butt." She taught me how situations of that nature should be avoided at all costs. Mama said, "Don't let any man get in the way of your paycheck!" She further advised, "There ain't that much love in the world."

Those encouraging words were affirming and noteworthy, but I still didn't know how I was going to handle Mr. Brown and enjoy going to work every day.

Chapter Five

Cold Shoulder

The weekend came to an end, and I felt empowered about how to handle Mr. Brown after ruminating over what Mama had taught me. She didn't come right out and call it "sexual harassment," because that terminology was non-existent at the time, at least to my knowledge, but it was a reality that was taking place across the globe and had been since the beginning of time. We as women just thought it was a way of life, something that we had to contend with in the many venues of our preyed lives.

Driving to work, I rehearsed the words I'd say to Mr. Brown and how in keeping it "strictly professional" we could remain focused colleagues guided by the same professional goals and principles. I desperately hoped we could pick up where we had been before that awful episode interrupted what I perceived to be our peaceful co-existence. Not only did I need the job, which was a career asset and boost to my self-esteem, but I wanted it. I looked forward to dressing up for work each day and the opportunity to grow in the political arena. I was so enamored with the world of politics.

I was the first to arrive in the office, which was an anomaly and triggered my anxiety. I turned on the lights, coffee pot, and copier to help get the workday started. As was customary, I got the furniture polish out of the cupboard, dusted Mr. Brown's office, rinsed his coffee mug, and opened his blinds. Then I dusted my own area and turned the jazz radio station on low in preparation for my day. I almost freshened my perfume out of habit, but the memory of our last encounter stopped me cold as I reflected on his comments about my "teasing him by looking and smelling good." I decided on THAT day to remove the "smelling good" component from the equation, but wasn't going to compromise "looking good" and chuckled at the fact that I couldn't, even if I tried!

"I'm going to always look my best, but I'll be doggone if he will EVER get a whiff of my cologne again. Not in this lifetime!" I thought, returning the Estee Lauder Youth Dew to my small leather purse and locking it inside the desk.

As our co-workers filtered into the office, I greeted them cheerfully while filing documents in the gray file cabinet. It was a new day and a new week, as far as I was concerned. "Let's let bygones be bygones," I thought. Just as I did with Daddy when he got out of pocket after too much alcohol, I planned to pretend the kissing incident never happened and hoped Mr. Brown would too.

The morning sped by rapidly and before I realized it, the time was 11:00 a.m. Mr. Brown usually got in no later than 10:00 a.m., or called to say he would be late. Today he did neither. This made me nervous. But I had plenty of work to keep me busy, so that was what I did. At noon, I took an hour off for lunch, and upon my return, his office door was closed. Mr. Brown had arrived. The closed door, however, meant Do Not Disturb, and I didn't.

Within the hour he came out, and his greeting was cold, formal.

"Good afternoon, Miss Thomas," he enunciated as he walked stiff-necked past my desk with nothing more to say. He was truly out of character, which saddened me. I sensed he still had feelings about what had happened between us on Friday and my heart sank.

"Oh MY GOD!" I cringed. "Why is this happening to ME? What did I do??!! He's the one that got out of pocket. Now that's a whole lot of nerve right there!"

I kept working and listened to how he interacted with the other staff members. He was his regular jovial, talkative self with them. I was the only one receiving the cold shoulder, or as Mama called it, "being fed with a long-handled spoon."

"That's all right," I thought. "If he keeps his hands away from me, I'm good. His behavior confirms that he knows he was wrong. I wonder, if I'd gone along with him, how far would it have gone and how would he be acting today? Probably the same way or worse. I'm between a rock and a hard place right now. Gotta ride this out and see what happens."

For the next three days, Mr. Brown was curt, abrupt, and downright cold toward me. At one point, I considered quitting my job. He was punishing me because he got out of pocket. Emotional abuse in the workplace due to sexual harassment is what that was.

There was so much tension between us. I even caught a couple of our female clerks whispering and looking in the direction of our office. I was certain they knew something was amiss. If I'd known then what I know now, I would have filed sexual harassment charges against him immediately. Not only because of the kiss but also for the mental/emotional abuse and insensitivity that I was experiencing. His behavior was making it impossible for me to come to work and do my job effectively for fear of retribution. It was all so unfair.

Gradually, over several days he began to be himself again and our working relationship returned somewhat to normal. I was glad, because his behavior had made the workday long and stressful. I was tired of walking on eggshells.

I believed our work life was good again on that sunny spring day when he walked past my desk en route to his office and said, "Hey you, wanna go to lunch today?" I breathed a huge sigh of relief.

Prior to "the sloppy kiss," we'd lunched together at least once a week. That was when he'd provide a full update on what was going on in and around the office. He viewed me as his confidante. I valued those times.

"Sure!" I answered gleefully. "Where to?"

He told me where to make the reservations, which meant we would walk there, enjoying the weather and small talk among numerous other employees going the same way. I felt somewhat assured and comfortable in doing that.

We laughed and talked as we walked, just like old times. I was hoping Mr. Brown wouldn't mention "it" and was relieved when he didn't. I got a little nervous, though, when the waitress asked if we wanted drinks. Just as with Daddy, I cringed at the possibility of dealing with another inebriated Mr. Brown so soon. I exhaled silently when he declined, requesting club soda with lime instead. Thumbs up, dude.

We began sharing a state of normalcy in the workplace once again and I gradually felt comfortable working with him. Eventually, I was no longer reluctant to enter Mr. Brown's office to deliver his mail, take transcription, or have him sign important documents, which placed me near him.

But I made it a point to wear high-necked blouses/dresses and left the perfume at home.

Chapter Six

Here We Go Again

The next time it happened, I was caught off guard. Again. We'd been working together well over the past couple months and gotten a great deal of work accomplished. I no longer felt nervous and believed we were rebuilding a healthy work relationship.

Mr. Brown still had his days when returning from lunch reeking of alcohol, but I didn't care. If he didn't bother me, it didn't matter how much he chose to drink. In the earlier days of our acquaintance, I tried to dissuade him from consuming so much alcohol during the workday, which might have created the misperception that I had feelings beyond the workplace. But now I adopted the attitude that drinking lunch was his business and I was minding mine.

I was still leery, but that was generally the case with all men beyond the platonic. My father set that tone and I rarely, if ever, let my guard down around them. I still enjoyed male attention and often basked in its abundance, but only trusted it from afar or with limitations. However, after Karl suggested that I had a tendency to send subtle mixed messages to men, it further inhibited me.

Early in adulthood, I began blaming myself for unsolicited advances from men. It appeared that they reaped few consequences for their predatory nature against women, who can be vulnerable to men and, at the same time, oblivious to that fact. Sometimes we flaunt our sexuality subliminally and get surprised when it is reciprocated. Few women will admit to that; I, however, knew I was flirtatious, but I was basically confused about how I should respond to men. But I didn't believe I was teasing my boss or soliciting his lewd behavior. And I still don't!

On this day during the Christmas season, he took an exceptionally long lunch. When he called to check in, he was so drunk that his words slurred. I could hardly understand what he was saying. What I could decipher, though, was that he was ashamed to come back to the office in that condition and needed me to bring his briefcase and wallet that were left on his desk. He had scrapped plans to return to work that day.

I informed the staff that I had to deliver his belongings and would be back shortly. Upon my arrival at the restaurant, his buddies left him alone and returned to work. I inherited the responsibility of trying to sober him up, so he could drive his car. Mr. Brown was in no condition to even walk a straight line, let alone drive. A déjà vu experience hit me hard as I recalled a similar incident with my daddy and got annoyed, thinking, "I did NOT sign up for this!"

Mr. Brown was SLOPPY DRUNK!!! I was embarrassed for him, not just because he was a public official, but also because he was my friend. At the same time, I really felt put upon because this was my boss and it was very hard to respect him at that moment. Mama always said, "a drunk ain't SH@#," and that was what I was feeling right then. The liquor had him feeling totally uninhibited, but being the enabler that I was, I felt inclined to protect him from public scrutiny. The high-end restaurant that was frequented by state and national political figures was filled with patrons who, outside of their own celebratory jubilance, kept looking over at his table.

After about an hour and a half of pouring coffee into him with gradual results, I called the office to say I would be gone for the rest of the day. My coworker kept asking about Mr. Brown (they'd worked with him for many years and knew him far better than I did) but I would not confirm what they already knew.

Gradually, I was able to get him sober enough to walk to the bathroom alone, rinse his face, and fix his clothes. When he returned, he was still slightly inebriated but not excessively. He stood by the table and thanked me for coming to help him get himself together. He then asked if I would follow him to our other office several miles away to deliver important and time-sensitive documents. Nervously, I looked at my watch, realizing it was 6:30 p.m. and Karl would be very upset that I was so late. I wasn't in the mood to fight with him but could not leave Mr. Brown like that. The last thing he needed was a DUI or negative publicity.

So I agreed to follow him, realizing it would be almost 8:00 when I got home. As I drove, I tried to think of a story to tell Karl because he was already very suspicious of our working relationship. I tried to mentally prepare myself for what would probably be a long night of arguing and fighting because he would not understand this.

When we got to the office, I planned to wait in the car, but he beckoned for me to come in just in case security stopped him. Reluctantly, I got out of my car, walked in, joined him in the elevator, and got off on the third floor. I held the bag as he unlocked the door and together we walked inside the dark office, where the horizontal window blinds were drawn. The security guard was not around.

I had barely put the briefcase down when he nudged close with fondling hands and wet, passionate kisses. His erection was pulsing against my thigh, but his grip was so strong that I could not pull away! He started grinding against me, grabbing at my crotch and breathing erratically with the smell of stale liquor. Then he grabbed my hair, snatched my head back, and yelled, "KISS ME, GIRL!"

Mr. Brown was using every ounce of strength to restrain me as I bit, kicked, and clawed my way loose! Every time I thought I was getting away, though, he pulled me back into him. I was so scared! I couldn't knee or kick him in the nuts, so I just stomped real hard on his foot with my high heel and ran toward the door!!! But amidst it all, I still didn't scream or holler out, because I didn't want to get him in trouble just in case somebody was within earshot—still trying to protect the **disenfranchised** black man. He tried his best to seduce me, but was too inebriated.

As I ran to the elevator, I was relieved to see no sign of him. Unsure whether I'd broken his toe or what and clearly not caring, I got on the elevator fixing my hair and straightening my clothes. When I got down to the first floor, the security guard was sitting there at his desk. I nodded and walked on out the door. He didn't say a word and neither did I.

I broke down and cried when I got in my car, not believing what had just happened with me and my boss. How was I going to go back to that job? How could I ever look at him with respect again? Who did he think he was?! Better yet, WHO DID HE THINK I WAS?

When I got home, it was 8:00 p.m. I hadn't thought of calling home to say I'd be late. Karl was LIVID! I didn't say one word but just took off my clothes, took a shower, and went to bed in hopes that he didn't beat me awake. He didn't—THAT TIME.

I called in the next two days because I was sad. My dream job was becoming a nightmare. Christmas break was in just a few more days. I decided to wait until after Christmas to deal with it.

Our relationship was destroyed. Mr. Brown was quiet and humble. I was mean and evil. Not one staff member asked what was wrong with me. It was as if they knew and understood. Within the month, I submitted a transfer for another department. Mr. Brown denied it. I started missing days. He never asked me why.

Within two months, I resigned and moved to Lansing, Michigan, to work for the State Department in a position that Larry Leatherwood helped me acquire. He and Joel Ferguson became my mentors and helped facilitate my acclimation to the greater Lansing area. Together, they became my mentors and breathed new professional life into my wounded spirit.

CHAPTER SEVEN

Corporate Blues

When I first laid eyes on the handsome, light-brown *Adonis*, walking tall and proud as if he owned the corporation, my eyes remained affixed to each stride he took, smiling and waving to our co-workers along the way.

"Who is THAT??!!" I wondered as I reached over to answer the ringing telephone. As I talked, my head turned, watching his handsomeness until he was out of sight. "Hmmmm. Now THAT's the finest thing I've seen since I've been in Lansing. He looks so professional and polished. Just the kind of man I need."

That was when I decided it was time to take a stroll to the bathroom and mosey around the very large office complex that clearly measured 25,000 square feet. It housed twenty secretaries, two assistant managers, twelve clerks, and thirty managers, whose plush offices were showcased by floor-to-ceiling glass enclosures. The outside walls were covered with beige brocade draperies. It was a very open area whose daily hustle and bustle literally flowed from sunup to sunset with visits from internal managers and outside business representatives. The phones rang incessantly.

I took slow but deliberate steps in trying to find His Handsomeness and as I rounded the outside corner, we almost bumped into each other. We both chuckled from being startled and almost said "excuse me" at the same time. The ice was broken but I kept walking, a little faster this time because I felt embarrassed and caught off guard by the sudden exchange.

As I continued my journey of discovery, realizing the massiveness of the twelve-story executive tower, I pinched myself to remember that I was a part of a worldwide organization. I rode the escalator as far as I could and then took the elevator to the top floor, which was beyond plush and lavish. That was where the big fellas worked! I was only slightly impressed as my encounter with Mr. Handsomeness kept me enthralled.

"The next time we meet, it will be easier," I whispered as I pushed random elevator buttons for lower floors where we commoners worked.

It was my second day on my new job with the Big Ten Company, and like him, I was the only African American on our huge team. The only visible difference between us was gender. As the premier blacks who broke the color line in our department, we would become kindred spirits. The year was 1977 and institutional racism was still alive and well in corporate America. It was there that I learned about the existence, reality, and definition of the proverbial "glass ceiling."

In addition to being the sole black female, I was also the youngest executive secretary on staff, so my skills were fresh and innovative. Since it was not my first stint as the singular African American amidst a sea of white people, I was well versed at presenting stellar people skills and demonstrating an impressive, high-level skill set. It mattered not if I was despised or not; I was respected among my peers.

In taking note of the unspoken dress code, I made sure my physical presentation was spot on as well, making monthly visits to Jacobson's, Lett's Fashions, and Ganto's Department Store to keep my suit collection up to par. I enjoyed dressing for my role as corporate secretary each day and looked forward with great anticipation to support this world-renowned organization with the same level of professionalism that I'd previously held. The only difference was the genre and the politics.

In the political office, the political games were overt and expected; however, in corporate America, I soon learned that the climate was equally political but subtle. The emphasis there was on profit and product—things more than people. But if you weren't careful in the corporate structure, you'd miss the message that learning "the game" was just as important if not more so than working for the politician. Consequently, it took me longer to learn that there was a game and how obscure the rules were.

My work ethic was intact. I was conscientious and determined because that was my personality; the work ethic I'd developed as young as six years old helping Mama clean business offices on Saturday mornings taught me to do my best and move quickly with intentionality. That was why I was able to assume my own private-duty home by the time I was twelve years old. A year later, I started washing dishes at the Te-Khi Truck Stop every weekend, and I kept both jobs until graduating high school seven years later.

But men were always my weakness, from boys to men. I liked them and had not learned yet to make them my dessert and not the main dish. It proved to be a hindrance to my career, personal success, and overall happiness through the years. I'm sure it confused onlookers who wondered how I could be "so smart and well-put-together" but couldn't quite figure out what my stronghold was. I had major "daddy issues" and that mysterious "itch."

The next time I saw *Adonis* was at my first staff meeting. It was held in the corporate auditorium. Our department was that big! Although we sat theatre-style, I noticed him immediately and positioned myself to sit within his peripheral vision, but several rows behind. He would have to walk past me to enter and exit. My intention was to remain seated when the meeting ended so I could also people-watch to further acquaint myself with our workforce. I wasn't feeling nervous, just brand-new and uncomfortable. It's not easy being green…

The meeting was about quality control, which bored me to tears. It was based on the W. Edwards Deming philosophy and this guy named Joseph Moses Juran, a Romanian-born American engineer and management consultant. He talked incessantly about organizational commitment to implementing a philosophy/practice for quality. He was considered the "evangelist for quality and quality management." It was far too technical for my blood. I would have enjoyed watching paint dry more than the torment of the long two-hour meeting.

The corporate culture was a far cry from the political environment, which I considered much more vibrant and people friendly. There was something about the corporate ambience that felt cold and impersonal, but the money and benefits were great. I made myself tune in and take interest in what was being said since I planned to be there for a while. It wasn't easy, though. I kept my eyes on Adonis, which helped me get through the meeting.

As I sat there among the sea of white faces looking all stuffy and stoic, my memory flashed back to the early days at LaMora Park. We were children then, but I wondered how many had conformed to a work environment such as this. It was then that I realized the benefits of learning to acclimate to the white world. For once, I didn't feel disdain for having to endure that nightmare.

It was then and there that I finally reconciled my resentment toward my parents for forcing me into that situation. The epiphany created a sense of gratitude toward them for moving our family into a racially segregated community and school. It had prepared me for moments like this and a few others throughout my young adult years. It was now 1977 and only fifteen years earlier I was fighting for my identity. Although the "struggle" continued, I realized that the Voting Rights Act had passed within that fleeting period. Those thoughts and memories carried me through the remainder of the meeting.

Periodically during the week, Adonis and I would cross paths in the copy room or walking to and from the parking lot. We'd engage in small talk that helped us get acquainted. But it wasn't until I attended the monthly Black Corporate Employees' Party that we struck up a real conversation. I soon learned that although Adonis was a good-looking man, he was square and uptight. He thought he was cool and suave, though, which humored me. My heartthrob, whose name, I learned, was Richard Rectangle, tried to exude an air of importance and superiority, a corporate persona, even outside the office setting. In retrospect, Mr. Rectangle was weak, full of himself, and superficial.

He danced like there was a stick up his butt and he had this fake laugh. But I still liked him. Dicky Rectangle was a far cry from any man I'd ever encountered through the years. As we got better acquainted throughout the night, I was encouraged by his obvious interest in me as well and believed my life would have taken a different path if I'd dated the square, studious guys early in life instead of the super-cool superfly types.

The hipsters only broke my heart and left me jaded with post-traumatic stress disorder. I had to pinch myself as I was having clean fun with professional people. I felt safe. There was no need to watch the door and beware of hustlers or hoodlums carrying guns, looking for a fight or trying to run game. I was finally crossing over into a destiny moment that was designed for me. As I observed the roomful of black employees from the five corporate plants within our region, I was pleasantly surprised that there were so many of us partying together with one accord.

As the lights came on and the party ended, one of the brothers in upper management spoke in the microphone, welcoming/introducing the new employees and thanking everyone for coming. He announced that the after-party was at his home and everyone was invited. As a twenty-three-year-old young, single woman, I was full of energy and had no interest in going home, so I decided to extend the evening and get better acquainted with my new co-workers.

So many people were introducing themselves to me that I immediately felt welcomed and accepted. Mr. Rectangle, who suddenly appeared out of nowhere, asked if I was going to the after-party and seemed excited that I was. I tried to be cool about it, but butterflies started fluttering inside my stomach at the thought of us partying into the wee hours of the morning together!

Although we danced with other people, Richard Rectangle kept coming back to me. On a few occasions when I saw someone coming my way I positioned my stance so I could be within his arm's reach instead of theirs and kept my gaze affixed to his. That was my way of saying "In case you're wondering, I choose you!"

He wasn't the smoothest dancer but he thought he was, which made it all the more enjoyable. But he liked to have fun and had finally loosened up. As the song says, "I could have danced all night."

As guests began vacating the dance hall, I went to the ladies' room to freshen up with a wet wipe, cologne, and make-up. The clock on the wall reminded me that the evening was still young with many possibilities. It was 12:30 a.m. and I was good for a couple more hours, at least.

I felt excited with hope and anticipation that something good was about to happen. I'd only been in Lansing, Michigan, for six months and although I was twenty-three years old, there was a whole new world awaiting me. For one, I didn't have to watch my back for some gun-toting fool to crash the party or a bunch of maniacs to start a life-threatening fight. Nor was I confronted with jealous, classless women who were envious of my natural persona.

I was among black urban professionals who had attended college or trade schools and were groomed for success. From what I could see among this crowd, there were no hood rats or ghetto-fabulous perpetrators here. I breathed a big sigh of relief and whispered a "thank you, Lord" prayer before exiting the ladies' room for new possibilities.

Chapter Eight

Tear the Roof off the Sucker

Aside from a few stragglers, the hall was relatively emptied of the revelers who I hoped were going to the after-party.

I took quick, deliberate steps to my 1976 black Buick Regal, looking straight ahead with focus and deliberation in the darkness of the morning. It was a survival skill I'd acquired while living in the Creek, aka the Wild, Wild West. I generally preferred traveling solo, as I could come and go as I desired. There were still a few cars near mine and several guys were laughing and talking loudly. I cautiously proceeded, grabbing the Mace out of my purse just in case.

"There she is!" someone shouted. "The new kid on the block! Hey! We waited around to make sure you were safe and to help you find the after-party if you need it."

Wow. Now that was nice. I felt special and flattered as I walked closer to the car.

"Gee, guys! Thanks!" I exclaimed. "How did you know I didn't know how to get there?"

Everybody laughed, which eased the tension and connected us at the same time. There were four guys whose faces were not familiar, but the fifth was my *Adonis*! I wanted to bust out in laughter because I was so happy but kept my cool.

He spoke up and said, "When we were dancing, you told me you hadn't really learned your way around Lansing yet, so I decided to wait around and show you how to get there."

"Awwwwww! That's so sweet, Mr. Rectangle. Thank you!" I crooned obsequiously.

"First off, call me Richard, okay? And as far as getting to the party in one piece, we have it all worked out. I can ride with you and Donny will drive my car. If that's all right with you," he stated with hesitation in his voice.

"Sounds like a plan to me," I replied gleefully. "Let's burn rubber!"

Everybody laughed as we piled into the cars.

"You know that was really corny, right?" Dicky asked laughingly.

"Yeah. I'm prone to be silly and corny all bunched together sometimes. Actually, I'm kinda square like you are." I giggled.

"Me? Square?! How dare you!" he said. "You know I'm cooler than any of those dudes from Battle Creek, with their country, thuggish butts."

"You get no argument on that one," I confirmed. "It's a different kind of place."

From that point forward, we began developing a friendship, talking about where and how we grew up, hanging out, and small bits of non-threatening personal stuff, just enough to catapult a young friendship.

Of course, I could have driven all night and basked in his presence, but the drive was short. We arrived in no time. Cars were parked in the driveway and along the side streets.

Richard got excited! "Man! Look at all the cars! Everybody's here! We are gonna tear the roof off this sucka THIS morning!" He jumped out of the car and almost left me behind in his haste to party down. And that we did!

Throughout the wee hours, I danced and danced and danced and met many co-workers. I'd had no idea so many black folks were employed by the company. But around 2:30, music still blasting, my legs and feet began to run out of gas. It was time for me to go home. I downed the glass of wine, grabbed my purse, and walked quietly and surreptitiously toward the door, letting myself out into the hot, humid early-morning air. I inhaled its freshness that was tainted by hints of cigarette smoke.

There he was, standing down the walkway smoking a cigarette. He was the cleanest smoker I'd ever met because as we'd danced, I hadn't smelled one hint of cigarette smoke, probably because I was captured by his clean, fresh body scent.

"Leaving already?" Richard asked, flicking his cigarette and stepping aside so I could walk past him.

"Yes sir," I replied. "Just call me Cinderella. My clothes are about to turn into rags and my car into a pumpkin."

We both laughed nervously, strolling together.

"May I walk you to your car? It's too late for a lovely lady to walk alone," he said.

"Of course," I answered. "Thank you."

Hundreds of thoughts flashed across my mind as we walked quietly along the way. But I kept them to myself.

"Did you have a good time?" Richard asked.

"I sure did! I really needed a good party, too. It was right on time," I said. "Did you?"

"Yep. Our company parties are always nice. We have an excellent group of folks who know how to have an enjoyable time," he said. "I'm glad you could make it. Now you are officially one of us. No longer a newbie."

We both chuckled as I unlocked the car. He opened the door and I got in. Before I could thank him, he handed me his card and asked that I call when I got home. He wanted to make sure I made it safely. I thanked him and said okay, then drove away.

I looked in my rearview mirror and saw him watching my car until we were out of sight. As I drove out of sight, I screamed!

"Oh my God! He wants me to call him when I get home! How sweet is that?" I said to myself. "Okay now, Bettye, don't read something into this. It's just how decent guys do things. You're not in Kansas anymore, Dorothy, so just chill…"

I couldn't WAIT to get home, clean off my makeup, and put on my pajamas. It was 3:00 a.m. Generally, I didn't call men, especially during booty-call hour. I'd learned the dangers in doing that. But this was different, I rationalized. "I'm just going to call as he asked me to do, let him know I made it safely, and then hang up."

When I finally grabbed the telephone and called the number, there was no answer after five rings, so I hung up.

"Well, at least I called as I said I would," I told myself, trying to be nonchalant but feeling slightly disappointed. "He's probably still hanging with his buddies. Maybe I shouldn't have called so soon…"

I turned off the light and covered my head, praying for pleasant dreams…

Within the hour, the telephone rang. Although I can't stand to hear ringing phones, I always answer late-night calls in case of emergency.

"Hello?" I answered groggily.

"Bettye?" the voice said. "I'm really sorry to call so late and even more sorry that I missed your call, but I just got in. The fellas wanted to have breakfast, so I've been with them. I'm glad you made it home safely. Look, I'm not going to keep you because it's late, but may I call you tomorrow?"

I sat straight up in the bed! "IT'S HIM! Richard Rectangle just called my number and he's on the phone RIGHT NOW!" My emotions were in overdrive. "And he's apologizing not only for calling so late but explaining why he wasn't available for my call! How special is THAT?!"

"S-s-sure, Richard. Tomorrow is fine. Thanks for calling," I answered. "Bye, bye."

Our brief exchange stimulated me so that I couldn't get back to sleep. Vain imaginings in the recesses of my mind kept surfacing. "What will we talk about?" "I should have asked what time he would call but that would sound too anxious…" "Should I stay home from church, so I don't miss him?" "If I could just get back to sleep so tomorrow can hurry and get here…"

CHAPTER NINE

Tomorrow Begins Today

Although I didn't get much sleep, I woke up and got ready for church. I couldn't resign myself to stay home waiting for a phone call, no matter how excited I was about Mr. Rectangle. Praise and worship was what got me through each day, and that took precedence over everything and everyone.

But I was hopeful. Today had to be a wonderful day because the weekend had been nothing but. I arrived early to teach my Sunday school class for eight- and nine-year-old students, thanking God that most students were there on time. I'd prepared a lesson on Galatians 5:14–15 that teaches about the Fruit of the Spirit, which remained a favorite during the three years I'd been teaching. In my grab bag of instructional aids, there were various fruits whose first letter corresponded with the letter of Paul's teachings (i.e., peace=peach, love=lime, goodness=grapes, etc.). When the series ended, we would devour the savory fruit in a delectable salad mixture.

The morning worship service was equally enjoyable. At the time, I was a member of Reverend Graves's Baptist church, a small, country church whose music was old-school rich. The rousing choir fully complemented his down-home preaching style that often mimicked stereotypical pulpit antics that was part and parcel of the Missionary Baptist Church. It was okay for a season, but I was at the point where I needed more teaching and less preaching in my spiritual walk.

On the drive home, thoughts of the previous night crossed my mind. I wondered if Richard Rectangle had called and hoped he was just waking up. I tried to formulate in my mind what we would talk about, as our evening together had covered a lot of get-acquainted territory. But still, I slightly accelerated to get home sooner.

Admittedly, I ran from the car and up the stairs to my studio apartment to get in proximity of the phone whenever it rang. The clock on the wall read 1:30 p.m. I believed he'd not yet called and went on about my day, glancing at the phone periodically as if that would hasten his call.

When 6:00 rolled around, I began to believe he might not call, which was all right with me because it was now time to study for my accounting class, which would clearly encompass three to four hours. I was slightly disappointed, though.

As a full-time employee, I was taking a class at Michigan State University in pursuit of my bachelor's degree in business administration, and accounting was kicking my butt. I hated the finite details of ensuring every ledger entry was accurate; otherwise my books would not balance. It was difficult to erase the memory of that grueling day in the not too distant pass that I spent looking for one solitary penny. Upon finally finding it, I broke down and cried like a baby out of frustration and relief.

Amidst my study session, I glanced at the clock every now and again but kept my nose to the grindstone. I'd learned in my twenty-three years of life that things happen as they are meant to. At this point, whether he called or not was not as important as the time we'd shared. We'd broken the ice and partied together. He had my phone number and would eventually call it when it was meant to happen. I found comfort in that.

At 10:30, I shut it down, took my shower, and prepared my wardrobe for the work week. An hour later as I lay in bed reading my Toni Morrison novel, the phone rang. It was Richard apologizing for calling so late and explaining why he didn't call earlier. We didn't talk about much during the brief conversation that ended with "See ya at work tomorrow."

Now I was distracted from Toni as I tried to figure out "what's up with this guy?" I fell asleep trying to figure it out, but happy just the same.

Chapter Ten

And the Beat Goes On

At work it was business as usual. If I hadn't known better, I'd have thought our exchange over the weekend was a dream. He still walked around with his head held high and barely speaking. The only difference was when he did speak, a very slight smile came over his face, but still, not enough to write home about.

All the other black folks who'd attended the parties were friendlier and made it obvious that we shared a new connection. They spoke, called me by name, and responded warmly, but Richard Rectangle acted like he had that stick up his butt again.

I was confused and offended. Yes, my feelings were hurt. So I started ignoring him. Whenever he walked past my desk, which seemed to be more frequently, I looked in the other direction. I made him invisible. Two could play that game…

Near the end of the week, as I was walking toward my car I heard someone calling my name from behind. I stopped and looked around. It was Richard. I turned back around and kept on walking. That was when I heard his steps quicken.

"Heeeeyyyy! What's up, cutie?" he asked jokingly.

I looked over at him without missing a step. My expression said, "Man, PLEASE!"

"Why are you giving me the cold shoulder?" he asked ignorantly, hastening his steps to keep up with mine.

I didn't say anything. I just kept walking. "He'd better leave me alone," I thought. "Before I hurt his little some-timey feelings."

"Okay," he said humbly. "I know I've been acting weird. Let me call you later so we can talk about it."

I finally spoke. "Richard, I have class tonight and besides, whatever game you're playing, I really don't have the time. I don't know what your issue is, but I am not the one!"

"Look, I have a lot of personal stuff going on, Bettye. My wife and I separated two weeks ago and I'm staying at the YMCA right across the street from your apartment. I really need a friend right now. Please try to understand and not take it personally. I'm just all over the place. When you find some time, will you just call me, so we can talk?" he pleaded.

"I'll think about it," I snapped as I got into my car and drove away. But I thought about our exchange driving down 496-East, throughout class, and after class. "Poor thing… But wait! How does he know where I live?!"

You know I wanted to hear what he had to say, because I was crushing hard, but I needed more time to process everything. He'd recently separated from his wife. That spelled double trouble. That explained why he acted one way at work and another outside the office. Officially, he was still a married man and a professional on the move. Although he came with a different mess, I realized that my bad experiences were not geographically related; it was the nature of people. Mr. Rectangle had his issues just like everyone else. Did I really want to take on a giant rescue mission of this magnitude?

Wow. I was physically attracted to him, but he was married. Yeah, he'd said separated, but I'd learned the hard way that meant married and just taking a break in most instances.

Self-talk said, "ANOTHER married man, Bettye! Do you really want to travel that road again?"

Bettye said, "He needs a friend and he lives right across the street from me!!"

Self-talk's reply was, "When you play with fire you get burned. Don't be hard-headed!"

"But I like him, and I want him!" Bettye said. "He acts like he likes me, too!"

"Don't forget the Biblical scripture, 'As a dog returns to his vomit, so a fool repeats his folly,'" Self-talk reminded me. "Don't forget what you went through with Karl."

"This is different. He's an educated, professional man with a lot going for him, not your standard Battle Creek street hustler," Bettye rationalized.

"Same old song with different music," Self-talk admonished. "At the end of the day he's just a man, Bettye, and a lonely, vulnerable one at that."

I waited two extremely long days before finally calling him. He seemed delighted and I was relieved. We talked for three long hours. When the marathon conversation ended, we had a better understanding and appreciation for each other. Our friendship had officially begun, with one caveat: we couldn't reveal the extent of our relationship at the office. I was confused about that because it was strictly platonic, but he insisted, and I complied, failing to recognize my propensity for the clandestine.

That Friday night around 7:00 there was a knock on my door. Mr. Rectangle arrived with a bottle of Asti Spumante and a mixed bouquet of fresh flowers just in time for our dinner date. I'd rushed home from work, showered, and shimmied into my new red dress. I was looking and smelling real nice. I accepted the gifts and invited him to sit at the small, clothed, candle-lit table set for two. He asked if I needed his help, but I graciously declined my first-time guest.

We dove into the homemade lasagna, garlic bread, and salad as if there were no tomorrow, sharing laughter and conversation about how famished we were from the busy week at work. I was so grateful that the chairs were comfortable because we sat and talked, drinking Asti, until midnight. I had to remind him that it was getting late for fear that the wine and chemistry we shared would evolve into Booty-Call Hour. But it took everything in me to accomplish that feat.

Over the next few months many organizational changes began taking place. I was transferred to a new manager with whom Richard worked closely. It was a lateral move for me with greater opportunity for advancement.

What I wasn't prepared for though was his heightened paranoia about our developing friendship that had naturally evolved into physical intimacy. I believed I was dealing with our arrangement okay. He was helping with groceries and I did most of the cooking two to three times a week. Quite frequently, he cooked a delicious meal, then we watched television, played backgammon, and talked about work. We also made GREAT LOVE together.

My heart was vulnerable. I was falling in love. He was heartbroken about his failing marriage, which was looking like divorce, and missed his daughter, with whom he was very close. I never got the full scoop on why they parted, however. We were great behind closed doors, but we never went out together. Initially, I chalked that up to the work situation and his pending divorce. Over time, I felt less comfortable about the situation but remained silent. I had also been groomed for secrecy.

Within that first year, however, I was surprised with a promotion! I was elated, and my family was proud. When they came to town to celebrate with me, his promise to join us dissipated into a lame excuse. I was beginning to see a side of him that I did not like. After all I'd been through with men from the streets, I could not believe I was being played by this square but crafty shyster. But I loved him.

The dynamic of our working relationship was such that we could co-exist as friends and co-workers since I didn't directly report to him. I was the secretary to another manager who worked down the hall from his office. But the copier, snack bar, and coffee machine were on my end of the building, which was why he walked past my cubicle frequently.

On the other hand, his office was located near the women's lounge and main lobby, which placed me near his office every day. Sometimes, though, I went the long way to exit the building or visit the ladies' room to avoid walking past his office. As our friendship grew, I was more comfortable with keeping our work and personal interaction separate, but I still didn't like it.

While he was living at the YMCA, which had been about eight months, our relationship was consistent. He assured me nothing would change when he moved into his apartment, which was on the other side of town. I even helped him fix it up, believing I would remain a part of his personal life. We'd been together for almost a year.

It hurt deeply to realize that what we shared was built on convenience and proximity, because after he moved, our talks, the visits, shared dinners, and backgammon games ceased. The only constant was late-night physical encounters that never resulted in overnight visits, as it had in my place. When I confronted him about it, he claimed it was the stress of the divorce, assured me that I was still special to him and that things would get better. But they didn't.

I recall a specific incident that remains fresh in my mind. Coincidentally, we were both shopping in the Quality Dairy store at the same time and a co-worker was also there, making small talk with him. Upon hearing his voice, I headed over to say hello. Richard ran to another aisle, ducking down so I couldn't see him. I was crushed. Then I ran into our colleague, who said, "Hey, Richard Rectangle is in here too. Did you see him?" As we stood near the checkout counter making small talk, Rectangle quickly cashed out and slithered out of the store without so much as an acknowledgement. Yes. That stung deeply.

And the company parties that were frequently sponsored by the black employees he stopped attending altogether. He'd avoid me like the plague on the days leading up to the social events. His behavior was confusing me because when we initially connected at the party he was open and receptive and appeared interested. He was now behaving like what my mama called "chicken doo-doo."

At work there were additional organizational changes in place and I was reassigned to become his personal assistant. It would have been palatable if we'd stopped being intimate, but I was now in love, he knew it, and we shared a strong physical chemistry. Basically, I was at his beck and call during and after work. Women were calling him. Lots of them. Resentment welled inside me, as I'd been the one to help get him on his feet. I believed I was next in line, that we'd find a way of being together. He said so. I adjusted to the craziness of our clandestine affair and all along he played me. The workplace became unbearable.

To make matters worse, I'd missed my period and couldn't keep anything in my stomach, but I kept it to myself. As I waited that long week until my doctor's appointment, I was checking my underwear every day for the slightest spot of blood that never appeared.

CHAPTER ELEVEN

I Messed Up

Dr. Oliver Beamon confirmed my fear. "You're pregnant, Bettye. It looks like you're about four weeks."

I should have been happy, because not only did I absolutely love children, but I was pregnant by the man I loved. But in the depths of my heart, I knew he didn't love me. Richard Rectangle did not want me, bottom line.

So I was stupefied and crept out of the office dazed. It wasn't like I hadn't used protection, but I never trusted those damn diaphragms. They were difficult to insert, could only stay in place for six hours, and I never felt they were as reliable as the pill, which I couldn't take. I generally left mine in for twelve hours or more, which led to stubborn, recurrent yeast infections, but I'd conducted significant research on the life of sperm and feared this possibility. I knew that most sperm died within one to two days, but could survive up to five days.

I'd been pregnant before and was very aware of my body. I knew I was pregnant within the first week of conception because my breasts were tender, and I had heartburn every day. Besides, I was "fertile Myrtle" and was known to be the person that if "it" could happen to anyone, it would happen to me.

As I drove back to work, I reflected over my life. I was twenty-four years old, certainly old enough to take care of a baby, and had an excellent job with great benefits. I wasn't married or in a committed relationship, but I'd known that when I'd lain down. BUT I was now pregnant by my boss, who wasn't my boss when our relationship began. What a mess!

"WHAT'S UP WITH YOU, BETTYE?!" I screamed. "ARE YOU HOOKED ON CONFLICT OR WHAT? WHY IS IT THAT YOU LOSE

FOCUS ON WHAT'S IMPORTANT WHEN IT COMES TO A MAN? HOW MANY CHANCES DO YOU NEED TO GET IT RIGHT? YOU KNEW BETTER!"

Mama's harsh chidings haunted me. "The more I teach you, the dumber you get…" She'd also warned, "You don't shit where you eat."

She was right. This was dumb and so was I. Why didn't I make better decisions? Why did I keep making bad choices in men? Well, I knew that one, but when was this cycle going to end? "I must be crazy or have some type of learning disorder," I thought. "I need counseling. That's what I'm going to do, get some professional help."

Within the week, I'd found an excellent therapist and begun working with him. He told me I was co-dependent based on being the child of an alcoholic parent and I was an enabler. With consistent talk therapy, he committed to helping me work through many issues that impacted my personal and relational life.

Finally, I began to avoid Mr. Rectangle and was relieved as he continued that ridiculous dance of making me invisible because he, too, was out of my purview. I had much bigger fish to fry: a life-altering decision to make that was about me, myself, and I. Rarely did I answer the phone anymore, for fear it was him, seeking to satisfy his loins.

Since I was now his secretary, too, it was difficult to ignore him totally, especially at work. I was surprised we made it two days with fleeting interaction, but on the third day, the inevitable happened. He buzzed the intercom on my phone and asked if I could step into his office for a moment.

"Oh DANG!" I cringed. "The day of reckoning is upon me." I grabbed the heap of papers that should have been filed days earlier. Gratefully, my arms were so full that my face was barely visible. Immediately I walked over to the file cabinet inside his office and began filing.

"The filing can wait," he said. "Will you sit down, please?"

I placed the stack atop his file cabinet and sat in one of four chairs positioned across his desk, choosing the farthest so he couldn't hear my pounding, breaking heart.

"So what's up?!!" he whispered, flashing that big, beautiful smile. "You've been so quiet and distant these last few days. I've been calling you…"

Immediately, tears welled in my eyes. "Oh DAMN!" I thought. "Why's he being so sweet, acting like he cares?"

"Are you crying, Bettye?" he whispered, handing me a tissue and looking all around through his glass-enclosed office to see if anyone was looking. "What did I say? What's wrong with you?"

His kindness made me cry even harder. Richard really was a sensitive, caring person. So he got up and walked over to the door, closed it gently, and touched me on the shoulder in passing, positioning himself back into his seat of power.

As he waited patiently for me to gain my composure, I wiped my eyes, blew my nose, and said, "I can't talk about it right now." I looked up and thought I saw genuine concern in his eyes. Why couldn't he exhibit those feelings all along? Perhaps if I'd played harder to get, he might have. But I hadn't, and now look…

"Okay," he replied. "Well, you know you can talk to me about anything, right? I mean, you helped me at a time when I really needed it and I'll always be here for you. Whether we have a relationship or not, we are friends. Hey! Are you free tonight?"

There it was. What I'd been waiting to hear. We were friends. Billy Paul would have called us "Love Buddies." We'd spent almost every day and night together for the past six months but to him, we were "friends."

"I'm sorry, but I've got to study for a big test so I'm not available tonight. Raincheck, though?"

He nodded, and I smiled, getting up from my chair, and headed for the door.

"Thank you, Richard, for taking the time to talk. You've helped more than you know," I said, and walked quickly to the ladies' lounge before the teardrops flooded.

Later that evening while I was deeply engrossed in accounting homework, the telephone rang. Out of habit, I answered the phone. It was Richard, wanting to talk even though I'd told him I'd be busy.

"That's a lot of nerve," I thought resentfully. "I told him I wasn't available but he's calling anyway??!!! So SELFISH!"

"Bettye? I hate to bother you but I'm on your side of town and wondered if I could stop by to use your bathroom. You know how my stomach is." He laughed nervously. "I won't stay long but this cramping came on me so suddenly..."

"THIS MF NEVER COMES TO VISIT ANYMORE, IS ALWAYS BUSY SINCE HE MOVED INTO HIS NEW APARTMENT, AND NOW HE WANTS TO TAKE A SHIT IN MY BATHROOM?! He's got a lot of damn nerve!" I thought, pondering whether to comply or not. "I oughtta make him squirm like he's had me doing all these months. BUTTHOLE!"

But instead I said, "OK, come on."

Within seconds he was pounding on my door. I took my time to answer because I was laughing so hard. Besides, I was also being vindictive in a passive-aggressive way. I'd barely opened the door when he burst in like gangbusters and ran to the bathroom. I walked to my bedroom muffling my laughter, so he wouldn't hear me.

"Serves his butt right! Literally," I mused, and returned to my homework.

When he finally came out fifteen minutes later, the smell of incense wafting in the air, he sat in the chair across from me quietly. I looked up at him, surprised.

"What's up?" I asked, slightly annoyed that he'd interrupted my studies once again.

"We need to talk, honey."

"About what?" I asked, swallowing hard.

"Us," he answered.

"Us? Since when did we become 'us'? You define THIS as friendship, Richard." I intentionally spoke quietly, trying to remain calm. "I told you I have to study, but okay. Everything works on your timetable anyway. So since this is YOUR urgency and it must happen now, let's talk! FRIEND!"

CHAPTER TWELVE

Love Buddies

"See? So why does it have to be like that?" he asked.

"Because that's the way it is, Richard. It's always about you, always has been from the moment you realized I lived across the street from the YMCA and you'd left home. You needed the comforts of home, INCLUDING my bed, so you played on my vulnerability and took advantage of the situation," I replied, looking straight into his eyes without flinching. It was as if becoming pregnant by him opened my eyes in an empowering way. I no longer felt so needy or vulnerable that I held back my feelings. Frankly, right now, I really didn't give a damn.

"You're right," he admitted, which momentarily took my breath away. "That was wrong of me to take advantage that way. I really hope you'll accept my apology…"

He waited for a response. I had none.

After several seconds of silence, I asked, "So. Is that it? Is that what was so urgent that you had to use your bad gut to intrude and interrupt my studies?"

"Welllll…not exactly…" he said, lingering as if searching for the right words.

"Boy, have I got something for you, DICK!" I thought. "I can't WAIT for my turn to speak!"

He started with a litany about how kind I'd been to him and how much he appreciated it, especially when he was struggling to get back on his feet. Then he mentioned our work situation and how my "phone attitude was becoming problematic." Since he was now "my BOSS," he felt it was time to "re-evaluate" what we were doing. He wanted to discuss it "outside of work initially" in hopes of resolving "the problem" so it wouldn't "cause any further problems" that he might have to "take action on."

I glared at him through tightly squinted eyes because my emotional barometer shot from ten to one hundred within seconds. "NO, HE DID NOT!" my mind screamed. Momentarily I was at a loss for words. Then…

"What are you trying to say, DICK?!" I asked, enunciating his first name venomously.

"Hon…you know what I'm trying to say," he whined, squirming in his chair.

"No, I don't. SAY IT, DICK!" I insisted, still glaring at him with fiery eyes.

"Okay…" he whispered, clearing his throat. "I've got to break this off, now. We cannot continue on as we've been going."

"Oh! You mean we can no longer be FUCK BUDDIES, DICK??! Here we are almost a year down the road and now that you are no longer on your knuckles living like a BUM in a raggedy room at the YMCA, using the comforts of me and my home, you're through??!! JUST LIKE THAT, HUH?" I whispered out of clenched teeth. "You used me, dude, and I really do not appreciate THAT!"

"Why are you making this so hard, Bettye?" he asked, reaching for my hands. "I fell for you from the moment I first saw you. I wanted you and came after you, but this divorce has really taken its toll on me. We came together out of mutual need and desire. You're right! You helped me through a very low time and I appreciate it more than you know. That was okay, if we were co-workers, but now that I'm your supervisor, we cannot continue down that road. It complicates our work relationship when you are mean to women who call my office or stop speaking when I talk to one of them too long on the phone! I can't live like that, Bettye, and I won't! Just because we've slept together doesn't mean you own me!"

A raging fire flashed from my eyes!!! My sharp tongue was now prepared for slicing…

"OWN YOU? I'M IN LOVE WITH YOU! YOU ARE THE ONLY MAN IN MY LIFE! I'M AT YOUR BECK AND CALL. I'VE MADE MYSELF TOO AVAILABLE TO YOU, MAN! WE JUST HAD SEX LAST WEEK, NEGRO! YOU DIDN'T THINK ABOUT ME BEING YOUR SECRETARY THEN! YOU'RE SO DAMN SMART THAT YOU DIDN'T EVEN WEAR PROTECTION, MR. BOSS MAN! THAT WAS STUPID, AND YOU'VE BEEN SCREWING ME FOR MONTHS WITHOUT USING ANY! WHAT MAN IN HIS RIGHT MIND LAYS UP WITH A WOMAN FOR ALMOST A YEAR WITHOUT EXPECTING EMOTIONAL ATTACHMENT FROM HER? YOU KNOW I'M IN LOVE WITH YOU BECAUSE I TELL YOU REPEATEDLY, EVEN KNOWING THAT YOU DON'T LOVE ME BACK! WELL GUESS WHAT? I'M PREGNANT!!! DID YOU HEAR THAT, MR. BIGSHOT? I. Am. Pregnant. With. YOUR. CHILD! NOW…GET THE FUCK OUTTA HERE BEFORE I CALL SECURITY AND HAVE YOU REMOVED!" I screamed as I walked over to the door and held it open for his exit.

Richard Rectangle sat in my chair staring at the floor looking dumbfounded. Then he looked up at me in shock. I smiled and beckoned "come here" with my finger for him to GET THE HELL OUT! He crept slowly to the door and exited with his head down.

"MOTHERFUCKER!" I shouted, slamming the door behind him. "NEXT TIME, FIND SOMEPLACE ELSE TO SHIT! YA DICK!"

The flow of hot tears finally released as I fell to the floor, crying uncontrollably.

Chapter Thirteen

Do What You Want, But Be Who You Are

Within the hour, my telephone was ringing off the hook, but I didn't answer. I was studying for my exam and besides, I figured it was Richard. I did not want to be bothered.

The next few days at work were tense. I was reserved, distant. He was obsequiously attentive, and it sickened me. Too little, too late as far as I was concerned.

I regret not being able to share the news about my pregnancy differently, but he'd been so consumed with basking in his new bachelor life and status as my "boss" that he was unapproachable. I needed to let him know, so I seized the opportunity. The ball was now in MY court.

On Friday morning, he stopped by my desk, whispering if I was available during the weekend, so we could talk. I told him flatly, "NO," hoping he'd ask again. Within a few days he asked again and I told him I had a lot going on but would TRY to make time. He seemed pleased and the tension that his face had been wearing since I broke the news softened somewhat.

"How about Sunday?" he asked nervously. The DICK was almost humbled. It amused me. "Like 5:00 p.m. I'll prepare dinner. Let's talk about this like adults."

"Okay. Sunday might work. I'll let you know," I answered, and returned to my typewriter as he stood there awkwardly. "You can go now," I thought. "We have nothing more to say unless it's work related." Finally he left as I turned to answer that darn ringing phone. I was so irritable lately.

Quite naturally, I got EXTRA CUTE for our dinner meeting and wore my best perfume. "Might as well mess with his head while I'm at it," I thought. All the while, I was envisioning our conversation that I believed might center on an abortion because he was a gutless S.O.B., obsessed with his image. I believed I was emotionally prepared after speaking with Mama, who reminded me that I'd already had one abortion and there was no reason to go down that road again. She was right, as usual.

He answered the door wearing shorts and a T-shirt covered by a chef's apron, smiling and holding a spatula. Cute, but not cute enough. Instead of joining him in the kitchen or offering to assist, I sat down on the couch and began reading the newspaper; ignoring his charming antics. An old song by the O'Jays, "I Dig Your Act," came to mind and I started humming it.

But he was relentless. "Hungry, hon?" he asked. "There's some hors d'oeuvres in the refrigerator if you want to get them out."

"No. I'm good," I responded, engrossed in the news article and relieved that I'd eaten before leaving home. I was enjoying his efforts to lure me in and reveling in my new strength even more.

Dinner was delicious. He complemented it with a vintage wine I'd never heard of, nor tasted. Admittedly, it did help me relax. I looked at the label that read 18% alcohol content, hoping one glass wouldn't hurt my baby. I didn't finish it, though, leaving the glass half-full, not half-empty.

We shared conversation and a few laughs before he abruptly jumped on the issue.

It didn't take long before the DICK went right in.

"You cannot have this baby, Bettye. I've only been divorced a few months and it will look like an adulterous affair interfered with my marriage. We both know that is not the case," he stated poignantly.

"This is not just about you, RICHARD!" I said quietly, looking into his eyes.

"Besides that, we are no longer just co-workers. You report to me. I am your direct supervisor, your BOSS on your JOB, your LIVELIHOOD where you are an AT-WILL EMPLOYEE," he boasted, placing strong emphasis on key words. "You are my secretary. Are you understanding what I'm saying to you?! Have you tried to imagine what that will be like? I have, and it's not a pretty picture. I'm sure you will say we should have thought about that at first, but that's hindsight. What's done is done. We MUST move on from here. We are NOT going to be together, so don't think that having this baby will hold me. IT WILL NOT! I've just left a family and I'm NOT taking on another! Understand?!"

I glared at him amidst the long silence. He did not look away but kept his gaze affixed to mine. Not only was he playing hardball, but this DICK was serious, ruthlessly so. Right now, I hated him and wanted to vomit every morsel of his funky dinner all over his cheap yellow plastic kitchen table. But I had no words. NONE.

I asked to use his bathroom, calmly got up, stuck my finger down my throat, and threw up all over his toilet, sink, and bathroom floor. Upon returning to the kitchen area, I asked for a drink of water, swished my mouth, and spat into his kitchen sink as he stood there in disbelief. Although I was tipsy from the wine, I was not drunk. I knew exactly what I was doing, intentionally.

And then I walked unsteadily out his door, closing it gently behind me. This time there were no floodgates.

"AFTER ALL I'VE DONE TO HELP YOUR BLACK, UPPITY ASS! YOU ARE THREATENING MY LIVELIHOOD, NEGRO?!" I yelled. "GRRRRRRRRR!" I was blind with rage.

Chapter Fourteen

The Last Supper

Hot tears challenged my vision as I walked slowly down the three flights of stairs toward the car.

"That wine was potent!" I slurred. Just as I neared the sidewalk, my heel got stuck on the fifth step from the bottom, causing me to trip and tumble down the remaining stairs. I hit the cement HARD and desperately tried to brace the fall and protect my belly, but it didn't help. Lying flat on my stomach, I writhed in pain and started vomiting profusely. I hurt so bad that I couldn't holler for help.

Suddenly, a piercing pain grabbed my gut severely and I felt a gush of hot fluid from my vagina. Initially, I thought I'd peed on myself, but when I reached down to catch it, my bloody hand signaled otherwise.

"Oh no, little baby!" I whispered. "Please be okay. Please be OKAY!"

It took several minutes for me to garner enough strength to get up. I was crawling toward the car when a man was pulling into the parking spot beside mine. He jumped out the car and ran over to offer help.

"Are you okay?" he asked, bending down to pull me up. I looked down to see how much blood was down there and sat back on my legs, pulling my dress over my scratched-up knees so he couldn't see it. I was so embarrassed!

"Come on now," he urged softly. "I've got you."

"No!" I shouted. "I'm OKAY!"

By then, he saw the blood on my hands and gasped. "You're bleeding! Did you know you're bleeding?! What's hurting you? Do I need to call an ambulance?!" he pleaded.

Ignoring his reaction, I reached out in silence, allowing him to help lift me up.

"I'll be okay, really. If you could just help me to the car, I'll be all right," I whispered, trying to be brave. The blood was now trickling down my legs and into my heeled shoes.

As the gentleman stood there in shock, I thanked him for helping me and grabbed a dollar from the cup holder, extending it with a blood-covered hand.

"WOW! Are you kidding me?" he cried. "Thanks, but no. Do you need me to follow you home?"

"No. But I appreciate you very much. Thanks for your kindness," I said as I backed up and burned rubber.

Chapter Fifteen

Raspberry Molasses

As I weaved through traffic toward St. Lawrence Hospital, thoughts of November 10, 1971, etched my mind, and I recalled the tragic day that my first baby died at my own hands. How could a mother take her own baby's life? What kind of woman was I? Now I'd killed another one. Yet I was a woman who adored children. I always had somebody's child with me. They were so innocent, pure and honest. I appreciated and valued children, believe it or not.

At that moment, I wasn't feeling good about myself. I knew I'd miscarried. It should have been me, not the innocent little baby. I was the one who wasn't fit to live. I should get rid of my own life instead of destroying innocent babies.

"Oh, little baby, PLEASE forgive me for putting your life in jeopardy," I groaned. "Dear God. Have mercy on me according to thy loving kindness, according unto the multitude of thy tender mercies, blot out my transgressions. Wash me thoroughly from mine iniquity and cleanse me from my sin. I acknowledge my transgressions; and my sin is ever before me. Against thee, thee only have I sinned and done this evil in thy sight… purge me with hyssop and I shall be clean; wash me and I shall be whiter than snow…hide thy face from my sins and blot out all mine iniquities… for I am but filthy rags. But Lord, cast me not away from thy presence and please don't take your Holy Spirit from me!"

The repentance was barely out of my mouth when scriptures began to flow into my spirit. God was speaking to me. "Trust in me with all thine heart and lean not unto your own understanding… Weeping may endure for a night but joy comes in the morning… To everything there is a season and a time and a purpose under heaven… He who dwells in the secret place of the Most High shall abide under the shadow of the Almighty… To everything there is a season, and a time and a purpose under Heaven… Fret not thyself because of evil doers, neither be envious against workers of iniquity for they shall soon be cut down like the grass and wither as the green herb. Delight thyself also in the Lord and he shall give thee the desires of tine heart!"

God spoke to me all the way to the hospital and upon my arrival, I was at peace. His divine favor was upon me, because I was received in the emergency room with urgency and efficiency. Within less than a half hour, I was examined by the doctor and released with the painful reality that my baby had died. Our six weeks together had ended tragically.

Chapter Sixteen

Retribution?

The story of MY sexual harassment in THAT workplace officially ended when my baby died, but words cannot describe how horrible the work situation became after that or how I watched as my boss, the DICK, romanced another employee, of executive status, in that same workplace and how they dated openly, eventually getting married and having their own daughter together.

I did, however, receive a semblance of retribution when, almost twenty years later, he left that wife for a blue-collar woman. For some odd reason, our paths crossed again, his abandoned wife's and mine. She was hurting deeply from his desertion and for a brief time sought solace through ME! That was when I learned that he'd told her that I "accused him of sexual harassment!" I told her, "I never did, but should have." I also explained to her that I would have been generously compensated for the emotional pain and suffering that followed our clandestine affair ending with pregnancy and miscarriage if I had sued him, but I didn't have it in me.

Not only was she astonished by my story, but she dropped out of sight after that. We had no further contact. I believe that was a divine connection where God allowed me the opportunity to tell my story and make an impact, albeit on only one person. She too suffered from his web of lies and deceit. In a small way, I felt vindicated.

Upon learning of multiple allegations of sexual harassment made against my eighty-two-year old hero, Congressman John Conyers, I felt his employee's pain unlike any other accusation I'd heard. It was then that I realized how both workplace encounters remained etched in my memory and the wounds had not healed. I knew then that it was time to tell my story.

I didn't share every account. That would take up too much space, but let me say this: there have been assaults from preachers, civil-rights leaders, and state legislators. Sadly, they all were black men. Not one form of harassment has emanated from a white male, which is my preferred work relationship of all.

For so many years I've kept it to myself, not wanting to embarrass anyone or cause pain. But my emotional reaction to this new movement of women, who suffered as I have and are speaking out, signaled their time was up, too. When the pain to conceal became greater than the need to reveal, the time had come. No longer will I carry their garbage. It's toxic for me, my family, and male/female relationships that I attempt to establish and maintain. After forty-three years of dragging their trash around, the time has come to relinquish it ALL. Tabula rasa means "blank slate." I'm clearing mine, right now and today. I'm tired now. Think or feel what you will. It's on you.

YOUR TIME IS UP!

CHAPTER SEVENTEEN

"THEIR TIME IS UP!"

On Monday, January 8, 2018, the nation watched television as media mogul Oprah Winfrey gave her acceptance speech as the first African-American woman to receive the Cecil B. DeMille Award at the 2018 Golden Globe Awards. As always, we were captivated by her beauty, style, and grace, but it was her eloquence, her carefully chosen comments, that made us tear up with pride in knowing her genuine concern for our plight as women trying to survive in a contrived man's world.

"The Cecil B. DeMille Award is an honorary Golden Globe award bestowed by the Hollywood Foreign Press Association for 'outstanding contributions to the world of entertainment.' The HFPA board of directors selects the honorees from a variety of actors, directors, writers and producers who have made a significant mark in the film industry. It was first present in 1952 and named in honor of its first recipient, director Cecil B. DeMille."

The award is presented annually, with exceptions being 1976 and 2008 due to a Writer's Guild of America strike. DeMille Award recipients have been predominately white males, except Sidney Poitier, Morgan Freeman, and Denzel Washington, all African Americans. Fourteen women been honored, however. They are Judy Garland, Joan Crawford, Bette Davis, Lucille Ball, Elizabeth Taylor, Barbara Stanwyck, Doris Day, Audrey Hepburn, Lauren Bacall, Sophia Lauren, Shirley MacLaine, Barbra Streisand, Jodie Foster, and Meryl Streep.

Oprah referenced the year 1964 and how with awestruck pride as a young child "sitting on her mother's linoleum floor in Milwaukee, Wisconsin," she witnessed actor Sidney Poitier walking across the stage to receive the 36th Academy Award for his role in *Lilies of the Field*. Winfrey recalls history taking form and marveled at "the most elegant man" she'd ever seen. She said, "his tie was white and of course, his skin was black."

"I'd never seen a black man being celebrated like that!" Oprah marveled. Winfrey added that "In 1982, as the first black man ever, Poitier also received the DeMille Award and recalls the explanation in Sidney's performance in *Lilies of the Field*; "Amen, amen, amen and amen." He, too, had received the Cecil B. DeMille award "right here at the Golden Globes…"

"At this moment, there are some little girls watching as I become the first black woman to be given this same award. It is an honor…and it is a privilege to share the evening with all of them…" The "amen" theme resonated throughout her historic comments regarding "this significant moment for women across the planet who can whisper those same words as the '#MeToo' movement evolves" into a much needed, long-awaited era of revelation and affirmation."

Winfrey thanked The Hollywood Press Association for its commitment to print truth. She recognized the press as being "under siege" at a time when their "insatiable dedication to uncovering the absolute truth that keeps us from turning a blind eye to corruption and to injustice."

"To tyrants and victims and secrets and lies, I want to say that I value the press more than ever before as we try to navigate these complicated times which brings me to this: what I know for sure is that speaking your truth is the most powerful tool we all have. And I'm especially proud and inspired by all the women who have felt strong enough and empowered enough to speak up and share their personal stories. Each of us in this room are celebrated because of the stories that we tell. This year **WE** became the story. But it's not just a story affecting the entertainment industry. It's one that transcends any culture, geography, race, religion, politics or workplace."

She expressed gratitude to all women "who have endured years of abuse and assault because they, like my mother, had children to feed, bills to pay and dreams to pursue. They're the women whose names we'll never know. They are domestic workers and farm workers, they are working in factories, they work in restaurants, they're in academia, engineering, medicine and science. They're part of the world of tech and politics and business. They're our athletes in the Olympics and they're our soldiers in the military."

And then she referenced the late Recy Taylor who died in late 2017, just ten days shy of her 98th birthday. Winfrey shared the story of a young Taylor who, in 1944, was walking home from church in Abbeville, Alabama. The young wife and mother was abducted and brutally raped by six armed white men and left blindfolded at the side of the road; threatening to kill her if she ever told anyone."

"Her story, however, was reported to the N.A.A.C.P. and a young worker by the name of Rosa Parks became the lead investigator on her case and together they sought justice. But justice wasn't an option in the era of Jim Crow. The men who tried to destroy her were never prosecuted. Recy Taylor lived as we all have lived, too many years in a culture broken by brutally powerful men. For too long women have not been heard or believed if they dared speak the truth to the power of those men."

"But their time is up," Winfrey exclaimed. "THEIR TIME IS UP! Their time is up. And I just hope that Recy Taylor died knowing that her truth, like the truth of so many other women who were tormented in those years, and even now tormented goes marching on. It was somewhere in Rosa Park's heart almost 11 years later, when she made the decision to stay seated on that bus in Montgomery (Alabama), and it's here with every woman who chooses to say, 'Me too.' And every man who chooses to listen."

She said, "In my career, what I've always tried my best to do, whether on television or through film, is to say something about how men and women really behave. To say how we experience shame, how we love and how we rage, how we fail, how we retreat, persevere and how we overcome. I've interviewed and portrayed people who've withstood some of the ugliest things life can throw at you, but the one quality all of them seemed to share is to maintain hope for a brighter morning even during our darkest nights.

"So, I want all the girls watching here now to know that a new day is on the horizon! And when that new day finally dawns, it will be because of a lot of magnificent women, many of whom are right here in this room tonight, and some pretty phenomenal men, fighting hard to make sure they become the leaders who take us to the time when nobody has to ever say 'Me too' again!"

Chapter Eighteen

The Second Annual Women's March

According to an Emily's List report, on January 20, 2018, "onlookers were met by marches and assemblies of several thousand women nationwide and the common chants were 'power to the polls' as thousands of women and men turned out to a national series of protests against U.S. President Donald Trump. The march marked his first year in office.

"The coordinated rallies in Washington, New York, Los Angeles, Chicago and about 250 additional U.S. cities and internationally featured speaker after speaker blasting Trump for policies that many said hurt women and urging voters to turn out for congressional elections in November." (Yahoo News 1/20/18)

National Public Radio's Leila Fadel reports "that…hundreds of thousands of people descended on Washington, D.C. in one of the largest demonstrations in U.S. history."

Although a big criticism was that the D.C. March was mostly "white, liberal women…this year organizers say they are reaching out to local partners after a year of grass-roots work to try to access a cross-section of America…" Many marchers "broke out their pink 'pussyhats' from last year in reference to Trump's "lewd remarks when he bragged about 'grabbing women's genitals' in a 2005 Access Hollywood recording."

A most prolific speech rendered by songstress/songwriter Halsey was rendered at the New York City Women's March and her hearty poem resonated:

"My best friend Sam was raped by a man that we knew because he worked in the Afterschool Program and he held her down with her textbooks beside her and he covered her mouth. Then he came inside her.

So now I'm with Sam at the place with a plan waiting for the results of a medical exam and she's praying she doesn't need an abortion and she couldn't afford it and her parents would, like, totally kill her.

"It's 2002, my family just moved and the only people I know are my mother's friend and her son. He's got a case of matchbox cars and he says that he'll teach me to play the guitar if I just keep quiet. And the stairway behind apartment 1245 will haunt me in my sleep for as long as I am alive. And I know I'm too young to know why it aches in my thighs, but I must lie, I must lie.

"It's 2012, I'm dating a guy and I sleep in his bed and I just learned how to drive and he's older than me and he drinks whiskey neat and he pays for everything. The adult thing is not cheap. We've been fighting a lot almost ten times a week. He wants to have sex and I just want to sleep. But he says I can't say no to him. This much I owe to him. He buys my dinner, so I must band him. He's taken to forcing me down on my knees and I'm confused 'cause he's hurting me while he says 'please'. And he's only a man and these things he just needs. He's my boyfriend so why am I filled with unease?

"It's 2017 and I'm living like a queen and I've followed damn every one of my dreams. I'm invincible and so fucking naïve. I believe I'm protected 'cause I live on a screen. Nobody would dare act that way around me. I've earned my protection eternally clean until a man that I trust gets his hands in my pants. But I don't want none of that, I just wanted to dance. And I wake up the next morning like I'm in a trance and there's blood. Is that my blood??! Hold on a minute…You see I've worked every day since I was eighteen. I've toured everywhere from Japan to Mar-a-Lago. I even went on stage that night in Chicago when I was having a miscarriage. I mean I Pied the Piper. I put on a diaper and sang out my spleen to a room full of teens.

"WHAT DO YOU MEAN THAT HAPPENED TO ME?! YOU CAN'T PUT YOUR HANDS ON ME! YOU DON'T KNOW WHAT MY BODY HAS BEEN THROUGH! I'm supposed to be safe now, I earned it.

"It's 2018 and I've realized nobody's safe long as he's alive. And every friend that I know has a story like mine. And the world tells me we should take it as a compliment. But there's heroes like Ashley, Simone and Gabby, McKayla, Gaga, Rosario, Aly, remind me this is the beginning, it is not the finale, and this is why we're here and that's why we rally.

"It's Olympians and a medical resident and not one fucking word from the man who is President. It's about closed doors and secrets and legs and stilettos from the Hollywood Hills to the projects in ghettos. When babies are ripped from the arms of their mothers. And child brides cry globally under the covers. Who don't have a voice on the magazine covers. They tell us take cover. But we are not free until all of us are free so love your neighbor, please treat her kindly. Ask her story and then shut up and listen. Black, Asian, poor, wealthy, trans, Sikhs, Muslim, Christian.

"Then yell at the top of your lungs. Be a voice for all those who have prisoner tongues. For the people who had to grow up way too young, there is work to be done. There are songs to be sung. Lord knows there's a war to be won. Thank you."

CHAPTER NINETEEN

"The IndyStar" — BREAKING NEWS

A key investigative journalist, Tim Evans, with the *IndyStar* newspaper said, "I've conducted somewhere around 10,000 interviews in my 40 years as a journalist, but one has been on my mind lately. It was my September 12, 2016, face to face meeting with longtime USA Gymnastics team doctor Larry Nassar." (investigations@IndyStar.com)

"The reflection was spurred by days of raw, emotional testimony…in a Michigan courtroom. More than 100 amazingly strong women detailed the physical and mental struggles they experienced after being sexually assaulted by Nassar under the guise of medical treatment.

"Their horror stories have been covered live on TV and spread across the Internet, attracting worldwide attention to what many are calling the worst sex abuse scandal in American sports. Nassar, a 54-year-old physician who also worked at Michigan State University, faces up to 125 years in prison. And whatever sentence he receives won't even begin until he completes a 60-year sentence handed down last month in a federal child porn case.

"I was part of the IndyStar investigative team along with Mark Alesia and Marisa Kwiatkowski, that first exposed Nassar's crimes in a story published September 13, 2016. To the best of my knowledge, I was the first--and still the only--journalist to interview Nassar about the sexual abuse allegations.

"Nassar came to our attention about a month before the interview. It was August 4, 2016. That was the day we published a story revealing USA GYMNASTICS OFFICIAL KEPT SEXUAL ABUSE COMPLAINT FILES ON SCORES OF COACHES but failed to report many of those allegations to law enforcement. It was part of an internal executive policy."

The newspaper was among "the top award winners in the 2016 Investigative Reporters & Editors contest, which recognizes the best watchdog journalism of the year." "The *IndyStar* received the Tom Renner Award for Criminal Justice Reporting for detailing the scope of child sexual abuse in gymnastics and the failure of Indianapolis-based USA Gymnastics to immediately report allegations of such abuse to authorities."

The judge said, "Without question, this series of stories was one of the most important and impactful works of journalism seen in recent years."

The rag's reporting "led to the arrest of a longtime USA Gymnastics national team doctor, the resignation of the organization's longtime president and bipartisan federal legislation co-sponsored by 16 senators."

CHAPTER TWENTY

A Gymnast Laments

"A decorated gymnast recounted the "eerie" environment at a USA Gymnastics training site during the sentencing for former MSU doctor Larry Nassar in January 2018. The Waverly Hills gym at Karolyi Ranch in Huntsville, Texas, has been used for many years as a training site for U.S. Olympic gymnasts, and has been mentioned by several gymnasts during Nassar's sentencing as a location where they were assaulted. USA Gymnastics recently announced the camp would no longer serve as the National Training Center.

"Mattie Larson, 25, was a member of the U.S. National Team from ages 14 to 19. She detailed isolated conditions, diet restrictions and painful injuries sustained at the camp during her victim impact statement.

"'There's an eerie feeling as soon as you step foot on the Karolyi Ranch,' Larson said.

"She said the camp was located in an isolated area and was an environment where abusers and molesters like Nassar could thrive. She said that 'during her time there, the pressure of competition and her abuse by Nassar led to depression, an eating disorder, and self-harm.'

"'From that first camp at 10 years old, I dreaded going back every single time for the next nine years,' Larson said.

Once, "to avoid going to the camp," Larson said she "splashed water on the bathroom tiles, laid on the floor and banged her head against the bathtub" to make it look like she slipped and injured herself. Her parents took her to the hospital to be examined for a concussion.

At the next camp, Larson said, Marta Karolyi told her another gymnast had fallen from her bunk and was still made to practice the next day.

"It makes me so sad to think about how desperate I was at that time," Larson said.

She went on to say that "the first time she remembers getting treated by Nassar was at age 14 for a hip injury at the U.S. National Championships in Minnesota. She continued to receive treatment from him until she was 19 years old.

"There was a camp where I sprained and dislocated both ankles at the same time," Larson said. "Larry checked out my x-rays saying I was fine. I was left literally crawling the rest of the camp."

She said Nassar was a renowned doctor, charismatic and "one of the only nice adults I had in my life at the time." Larson said Nassar would bring her "treats and junk food" when she'd been placed on a restrictive diet by coaches.

"I just couldn't comprehend that someone like him could do something so awful," she said. "On top of that, who was I going to tell? Certainly not my coaches, who I was afraid of."

Several other gymnasts have referenced Nassar's efforts to bring them food when coaches wouldn't allow it, a technique many believe was Nassar's way of grooming the young gymnasts.

Larson told the LSJ Nassar's favors eased the "prison-like mentality' of Karolyi Ranch."

"I absolutely would lose weight every single time and when I got back to my home gym. My coaches would be so happy," Larson said during a break in the hearing.

Larson has advocated for legislation that would make it a federal crime for Olympic national governing bodies to fail to promptly report child sexual abuse allegations to authorities. She met with Senator Dianne Feinstein, D-California, to advance the cause.

"All I wanted to do as a kid was go to the Olympics," Larson said. "I was at the height of my career at the age of 19 and the Olympics were just one year away. I just couldn't take any more abuse."

"I was broken. Larry, my coaches and USAG turned the sport I loved as a kid into my own personal hell," lamented gymnast Beth LeBlanc.

CHAPTER TWENTY-ONE

The Interview That Wasn't

According to journalist Tim Evans, "when we met in a conference room in Attorney Borgula's office, Nassar had a stack of medical books, magazines and a laptop. Before agreeing to answer questions on the record, Nassar asked to show me a video. He said it was one of many he had made for training purposes. He said he hoped it would help me better understand the medical procedure the three women had misconstrued as a sexual assault.

"The video focused on the backside of what appeared to be a young girl. She was lying down, wearing underwear. Nassar worked his hand between her legs, massaging the girl's buttocks and inner thighs. His hands slowly worked deeper into her crotch, but I never saw any penetration," Evans said.

"Nassar appeared at ease as he started to explain what he was doing. But the presentation was interrupted when my phone pinged with a text message that would end up derailing the interview.

"My colleagues' text confirmed a lawsuit had been filed against Nassar in California. The way I saw it, I had an ethical duty to tell the doctor and Attorney Borgula. With this new development, I asked, did they want to continue with the interview?" Evans said.

"Attorney Borgula asked for a copy of the lawsuit. I forwarded him a copy one of my colleagues had sent to me. Nassar and his attorney then left the interview room to review the new allegations from a former Olympian.

"I waited alone for about 15 minutes before they returned. Although the victim was identified only as Jane Doe, the background in the court record about her Olympic involvement was enough for them to know who she was. Nassar said he couldn't believe the woman would make such alle-

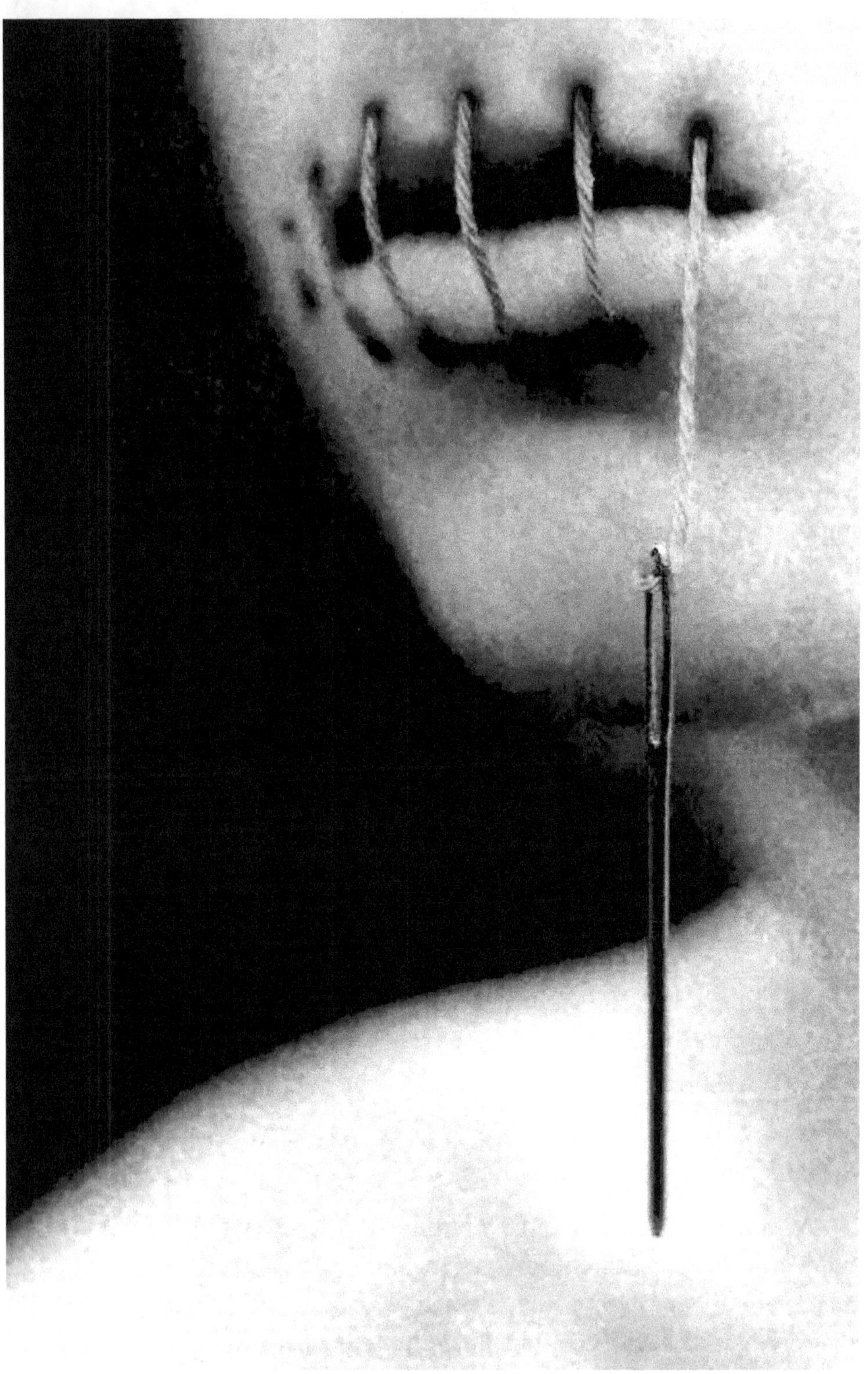

gations. He said he had a plaque in his office that she sent him as a thank you gift after the 20000 Olympics.

"In light of the lawsuit, Borgula cut off the interview. Nassar would not be allowed to talk, but the attorney said he would make a statement addressing the allegations.

"He denies all the allegations. He's never heard these allegations before. No one from law enforcement, any other regulatory body, USA Gymnastics, any individuals, parents – no one has ever suggested Dr. Nassar has done anything in any context with either this gymnast or any other that he's aware of. This is the first time anyone's ever made such an allegation related to USA Gymnastics," Borgula said.

Again, this would be proven wrong. Others had complained.

"Attorney Borgula and Nassar parted ways not long after our interview. The split came after federal authorities served a search warrant on the embattled doctor's home and found 37,000 images of child pornography," the *IndyStar* writer said.

"As I gathered my notebook and recorder, it was clear that the lawsuit rattled Nassar. His eyes were filled with tears and he was trembling as I shook his hand and said goodbye. My last memory of the encounter was Nassar pleading for me to be fair and to consider the harm a story could do to his reputation and family.

"After I left, I drove to a parking lot of a nearby office building and called back to Indy to share the little my interview had yielded," Evans added.

"Our story was published on the Internet that afternoon and in the IndyStar the following morning. We were bombarded with phone calls and emails from Nassar's supporters. They vociferously defended him, while questioning our motives, ethics and truthfulness.

"Here's one of many examples," Evans said. "I'm 150% sure that he is innocent, and I do not appreciate the one-sided reporting on this issue. Please, I urge you to look beyond making money by writing scandalous stories and consider the huge, unfair negative affect this is having on an innocent man's life. These false allegations bring me and my family so much sorrow. Please listen report on the plethora of people who are coming to this man's defense. By focusing on these false allegations, you're doing good to no one.

"Since then, more than 150 women have come forward to say Nassar sexually abused them. Many of those survivors are sharing their stories in the courtroom where Nassar will learn his fate," Evans said.

"And I'll be watching!" the writer concluded.

CHAPTER TWENTY-TWO

The Uneven Balance Beam

As the final gymnast to testify in an Ingham County Circuit Court Judge Rosemarie Aquilina's courtroom, Rachael Denhollander had this to say:

"What you have done makes my hate towards you uncontrollable. Larry Nassar, I hate you. What you have done is despicable. What you have done cannot be erased. I find more peace in knowing one day that you are going to die and when you do your pain will not subside. I want you to apologize to me right here. I want to forgive you, but I want to hear you.

"I'm not weak and I will not accept those feelings of embarrassment of shame. I'm leaving those here with him... You can see how so many victims were impacted by him…many of these women describe themselves as survivors. He had the gall to tell the judge during victim impact statements that it was affecting his mental health…

"You were not finished yet. You assaulted me again and again," she said tearfully.

Michigan's own Jordan Wieber said, "Larry Nasar is accountable. USA Gym is accountable. US Olympic committee is accountable. My teammates and friends have been through enough and now it's time for change because current and future gymnasts do not deserve to live in anxiety, fear or be unprotected as I was."

Finally, Nassar prepares for sentencing and rises to meet his fate before Judge Aquilina who gave him credit for 369 days served. Before sentencing, Michigan Assistant Attorney General Angela Povilaitis addressed Ingham County's 30th Circuit Court Judge with these comments:

"The breadth and ripple is infinite. It spans the State of Michigan, reaches across the United States and International communities. It's not even limited to gymnasts as athletes, but dozens of different sports also report abuse that spans 25 years. There were countless victims before he was doctor. Nassar's access to children ended when one brave women came to stop him. He penetrated vaginas…had erections as he performed so-called treatments on mere children. A twisted doctor who used his prestige leaving many emotionally shattered by a man that was trusted and loved. He is a master manipulator who tried to manipulate police and prior investigators, all the while knowing the truth; that he did what he was accused of doing.

"In gymnastics young girls do what they are told; to hide their pain and injuries. Their bodies are always on display and under scrutiny. It takes some kind of sick pervasion, not only to assault a child but to do so with parents in the room; to do so while young girls waited to see this doctor.

"This doctor gave basement treatments as his wife and children waited upstairs. Parents sat feet away not knowing. For Nassar, it was the thrill that he might just get caught. He was a master with a built-in defense… The trust he gained by being the Olympic doctor, one who treated young girls… he made his victim feel special.

"He often knew victims' parents, some who were fellow doctors who sent patients to him. Some were even police officers…He believed he was untouchable. He robbed the children of their innocence and robbed them of their good health. Some lifelong injuries could have been treated if he'd not wanted access to their young bodies. As one expert so eloquently said he was performing hocus pocus medicine. Did he really think he was going to get away for two decades?

"…I'm struck by the number of observations…What does it say about our society that victims have to hide their pain for years when they did nothing wrong? When victims do come forward, they are met with skepticism and doubt; treated as liars until proven true? These words will burn cultural stereotypes and myths. We must start believing. Other adults must believe our children. Believe regardless of who the perpetrator, regardless of his position. Research shows that false allegations are slim. If they are believed, supported and not blamed, we can protect other victims.

"There are still people in this very community who are saying that these women were in it for money or attention. Are you kidding me? After 150 raw, visceral statements?!! Even on this day there are still likely people who doubt. Anyone can be a serial sex abuser. Serial child molesters hide among us. This defendant had a good public persona. Good guy, goofy guy, medical school professor, gym god, religious man, school board candidate, husband, father, kind, giving, always approachable, saw patients anywhere, didn't charge for services.

"According to his strand, Nassar was a prolific child abuser. He spared no one. He lied. He hid behind the facade that people believed was real. People came to his defense. It was the man they wanted to see, but not the monster. He was confusing to women. He was so nice, gave presents, desserts, broke rules especially when contrasting his behavior against strict coaches. We must teach boys and girls to speak up, but when they speak nothing happens. Girls are taught to say silent when they should be allowed to be heard. Keep speaking up until someone hears.

"We need investigative journalists more than ever. That's what started this investigation. Without the reporting of The Indianapolis Star story in 2016, when Rachel came forward, he would still be practicing. Right now, Nassar would be at his office on Hagadorn Road and Hannah on MSU's campus had it not been for the investigative reporting and Rachel. We know trainers or coaches, or deans didn't stop him. Reporters began the story in excellent reporting.

"I am proud of the MSU police and Chief Jim Dunlap. MSU Sergeant Andrea Mumford was a smart, compassionate and dedicated investigator. Because of them the victims are fortunate. Our team is so proud of these woman for speaking up. They should feel not shame because they did nothing wrong. He did!

"One woman who came public was ridiculed. They tried to discredit her and believe him over her because of who he was reported to be. People supported him in this community. They chose to believe his lies over a woman who had nothing to gain by coming forward. Some support waivered as the child porno was revealed. They say he was framed and images were planted…It has not been an easy process for these victims, especially Rachel. You have seen first-hand, tangible physical evidence that women were abused. They are not bandwagon jumpers. Sexual abuse and assault alters victims' lives. It seeps and oozes at every core and alters the life trajectory causing depression, anxiety, suicidal ideation, self-medication and even suicide. Nassar sentenced these little girls by fear and doubt…abuse has turned their world upside down and inside out."

CHAPTER TWENTY-THREE

Michigan Judge Administers Justice

Once the abuse was discovered, several USA Olympics Team members jumped ship from the once prestigious board of directors.

Meanwhile, Ingham County Circuit Court Judge Rosemarie Aquilina, read excerpts of Nassar's cynical letter alleging the charges were "trumped up and he was being manipulated." "He concurs that although he'd participated in child porn for just a few months, he was sentenced to sixty years for the crime.

She says initially she "believed he might be innocent."

"This letter, which comes two months after his pleas, indicates he still thinks that he is right; that he is entitled and that he doesn't have to listen. I wouldn't send my dogs to you sir," Judge Aquilina said. "There's no treatment here, you finally told the truth. Inaction is an action. Silence is indifference. Justice requires action and a voice and that is what has happened here in this court… I want to be the voice on behalf of the survivors who asked law enforcement to continue along with the federal government.

"There has to be a massive investigation as to why there was inaction; silence. I applaud all counselors in the Attorney General's office and the defense counsel. You all have done fine work," she said. "You've made me proud of our legal system. We all work together for the betterment of our community. Law enforcement, investigators, we need this balance. So, all of you, when I look at myself, as lady justice, my arms are balanced. It only starts to tip afterwards and I consider everything that has happened. So, I want everyone to understand. I've also done my homework. I always do…I wanted all victims to speak. That was part of our plea agreement, to allow victim impact statements.

"Sir you knew you had a problem. That is clear to me. You knew you had a problem at a young age, before you became a doctor. You could have taken yourself from the temptation but did not. Survivors talk about how world renowned you were. You could have gone anywhere in the world to be treated. Any resort, any doctor, place where you could get treatment. You would have done that if you had cancer.

"You are about self-preservation, but you decided to not address what's inside you to control this urge that causes you to be a sexual predator. So, your urges escalated and based on the numbers that go unreported, I can't guess how many vulnerable women and children you have actually assaulted. Your decision to assault was precise, devious, despicable, manipulative. You can't give back their innocence, their youth. You can't return the daughter to the mother, the father to the daughter. You played on every vulnerability.

"I'm not vulnerable, not to you; to other criminals at that podium. I am well trained. I know exactly what to do at this time and I would like to do it," the Judge said. "I want you to know the honor it was to hear the survivors. It is an honor to sentence you. Because sir, you do not deserve to walk outside a prison ever again. Everywhere you walk destruction will occur to those most vulnerable. Now I am honoring the agreement…It is my privilege, on counts 1, 2, 5, 8, 10, 18 and 24, to sentence you to 40 years…that is 480 months," she announced.

"On the tail end, I need to send a message to the parole board that IF you survive 60 years in federal prison, then you start on my 40 years. Sir, I'm giving you 175 years…I've just signed your death warrant. I find that you don't get it that you're a danger. You remain a danger. I'm a judge who believes in rehab when rehab is possible. I don't find that possible with you. Credit of 369 days. Count 24 you will have 370 days credit. If you ever get out, you will be required to register with the Michigan sex abuse registry. You will pay restitution in an amount to be determined and submitted for the victims. I am leaving restitutions open as long as these victims have issues. You must submit to HIV testing…" she said before sounding the gavel.

CHAPTER TWENTY-FOUR

MSU President Resigns

Meanwhile, according to *Huffington Post* writers Sara Bouboltz and Daha Madani, "Lou Anna Simon resigned her position as president of Michigan State University on Wednesday, January 24, 2018," abruptly ending a thirteen-year tenure at the university's helm and in the wake of a massive sexual assault scandal involving the disgraced sports team doctor Larry Nassar.

"Calls for Simon to step down began with reports that MSU administration officials and law enforcement knew about Nassar's behavior and failed to stop him. Following Nassar's sentencing for sex crimes on Wednesday, a source told the MSU student paper, *The State News*, that Simon would step down from her position by Friday.

"Simon posted her resignation on the school's website, addressing the statements of Nassar's victims, citing that 'blame is inevitable.'

"I urge those who have supported my work to understand that I cannot make it about me now," Simon wrote. "Therefore, I am tendering my resignation as president according to the terms of my employment agreement.

"Simon told the *Detroit News* that she knew about the abuse allegations in 2014 – two years before Nassar was fired by the school – when a title IX complaint and a police report were filed. School police investigated but allowed Nassar to keep seeing patients. At least two student athletes had previously voiced complaints about him to university staff.

"'I told people to play it straight up, and I did not receive a copy of the report. That's the truth,' Simon told the *News*. The same article said that more than a dozen MSU staffers knew about the accusations of abuse and did nothing."

Michigan's two senators, Debbie Stabenow and Gary Peters, called for Simons to resign on the day of Nassar's verdict. Both Democrats are alumni of the university.

Senator Peters released a statement in which he emphasized the need for new leadership as MSU has a "long way to go in rebuilding trust."

Many of the women who read statements in Judge Rosemarie Aquilina's Lansing, Michigan, courtroom blamed MSU and USA Gymnastics for failing to act sooner. Several USA Gymnastics officials resigned prior to Nassar's sentencing. In an open letter apology to the Team USA victims, the US Olympic Committee also pledged to launch a third-party investigation into who enabled Nassar to commit his abuses for so long.

MSU faculty called for a vote of no confidence in the school's leadership the week of the trial, while *The State News* ran a front-page feature demanding Simon's resignation. Michigan Attorney General Bill Schuette plans to open an investigation into MSU's role in the scandal.

CHAPTER TWENTY-FIVE

"This is Survival"

American gymnast and two-time Olympian Alexandra Rose "Aly" Raisman said, "Everyone is a survivor of something. Everyone is battling something. Everyone goes through ups and downs in their lives. The hard parts are scary and uncomfortable to talk about, but they are part of the fabric of our lives. The tough times make us stronger and make us who we are.

"I've chosen to open up about my experience because I want change. It is very hard and uncomfortable to talk about. I have learned that everyone copes differently. There's no map that shows you the path to healing. On days I feel happy and protected for sharing my story. Other days I have bad anxiety and either feel traumatized by Larry Nassar's abuse or I fear something more will happen in the future. When I have these scary thoughts, I try my best to find things to help me manage my fears. I go for a walk outside. I read a book. I meditate and practice my breathing exercises. I take a hot bath. I draw. I hang out with family and friends. And I remind myself I am in control and that I will be okay.

"I also want people to understand that abuse is never okay. One person is too many and one time is too often. We must protect the survivors and people who are suffering in silence. We must support those who come forward, whether it is today, tomorrow, in three months, one year from now, ten years from now. Whenever it is, everyone must show support. Victim shaming must stop.

"Why didn't you speak up? Why are you just speaking now? Are you nervous? This will define you! To them, I ask that they consider how complicated it is to deal with abuse. Abusers are often master manipulators and make their survivors feel confused and guilty for thinking badly of their abusers. And the abusers also often make everyone around them stand up for them, leaving the survivor afraid that no one will believe them. That needs to stop. Those who look the other way must stop and protect those being hurt. The abuser must never be protected.

"The power needs to shift to the survivors. Sexual abuse isn't just in the moment. It is forever. Healing is forever.

"Soon after Larry pleaded guilty to federal child pornography charges, I was informed that I could submit a Victim Impact Statement to the court for sentencing consideration. If I wanted, I could also request to read the statement in court on the day of sentencing. Deciding to write the letter was a relatively easy decision. Deciding to read it in court, in front of Larry, was not easy. After some internal back and forth, I decided I wanted to go to the sentencing and read the letter. I submitted my statement and waited.

"It is up to the judge to decide if victims can read statements. I assumed the judge would allow myself – and the other five survivors who made the same request – to speak. I felt the judge would agree to have Larry listen to these survivors, to hear our stories about the harm he inflicted…not just in the moment but in their everyday lives. I wanted to be present to not only show him I was strong, but also to explain how his abuse still impacts me today.

"As the date of sentencing approached, there was still no word from the judge. Not knowing caused me anxiety. I needed to mentally prepare myself for speaking in front of this monster. I knew the court had my letter and I knew the judge was taking my statement under consideration when determining Larry's sentence. Around this time, Larry pleaded guilty to a number of criminal sexual assault charge. After Larry entered a plea, he was allowed to speak. This is what he said: '*For all those involved, I'm horribly sorry. This was like a match that turned into a forest fire out of control and I pray the rosary every day for forgiveness. I want them to heal. I want this community to heal. I have no animosity. I just want healing. It's time.*'

"He abused so many over the span of decades and *HE's sorry things got out of control?!* And *HE* holds no animosity?! Does he think HE is the victim??!

"I began to doubt if speaking in front of Larry would offer me any comfort. Seeing him would be scary and extremely traumatizing. One week before his sentencing, I was told the upsetting news that the judge had denied Larry's survivors an opportunity to speak. I was also disappointed that the other survivors wouldn't be given the choice to speak because they may have found it healing in some way…

"I am not a victim. I am a survivor. The abuse does not define me, or anyone else who has been abused. This does not define the millions of those who's suffered sexual abuse. They are not victims, either. They are survivors. They are strong. They are brave. They are changing so the next generation never has to go through what they did. There have been so many people who've come forward in the last few months. They have inspired me, and I hope, together, we inspire countless more. Surviving means that you're strong. You're strong because you came out on the other side, and that makes you brave and courageous.

"Now we need to change the cycle of abuse. We need to change the systems that emboldens sexual abusers. We must look at the organizations that protected Nassar for years and years: USA Gymnastics, the US Olympic committee, and Michigan State University. Until we understand the flaws in these systems, we can't be sure something like this won't happen again. This problem is bigger than Larry Nassar. Those who looked the other way need to be held accountable, too. I fear that there are still people working at these organizations who put money, medals, and reputation above the safety of athletes. And we need to change how we support those who've been abused. I want to change the way we talk about sexual abuse, and I want to change the way we support survivors of any kind of abuse.

"I didn't get to read my letter in court. But I don't want it to go unread. I've shared it with you below. This was one of the hardest things I've ever had to do. Every time I share my story, it feels like the first time. I relive years of trauma. But this is part of my truth and part of my healing.

"This is survival.

"*Below is the statement that I was prepared to read at the sentencing hearing:*

"Realizing that you are a victim of sexual abuse is a horrible feeling. Words cannot adequately capture the level of disgust I feel when I think about how this happened. Larry abused his power and the trust that I and so many others placed in him, and I am not sure I will ever come to terms with how horribly he manipulated and violated me.

"Larry was the USA Gymnastics national team doctor and the U.S. Olympic team doctor. He was trusted by so many and took advantage of countless athletes and their families. The effects of his actions are far-reaching, since abuse goes way beyond the moment, often haunting survivors for the rest of their lives, making it difficult for them to trust others and impacting their relationships. It is all the more devastating when such abuse comes at the hand of such a highly respected doctor, since it leaves victims questioning the organizations – and even the medical profession itself – upon which so many rely.

"I am writing this letter to share some of my story in hopes that it will help others understand the profound impact Larry's abuse had on me, how his betrayal of trust has changed me, and how his actions years ago continue to affect my daily life.

"From the age of eight, all I wanted to do was go to the Olympics. I loved gymnastics with all my heart, and worked as hard as I could. Larry, you knew how badly I wanted to be the best I could be, you knew how hard I worked, and that I would do absolutely anything to be on the team.

"You were my doctor and like most people, I was taught to trust doctors. I believed that you had my best interests at heart, and you made sure that message was reinforced, insisting your inappropriate touch was for medical reasons and that your care would help me get to the Olympic Games. You promised me that you would heal my injuries. You gave me gifts to make me think you were a good person, to make me believe you were my friend. You were nice so that we would trust you, it made it easier for you to take advantage of so many people, including me. But you lied to me. You lied to all of us.

"And because of you, I now have a hard time trusting other people. When I go to the doctor, especially a male doctor, I am scared and uncomfortable. Even if that doctor is recommended as the best, I am skeptical because I was told you were the best, and you certainly weren't. I am afraid that another doctor will mistreat me and abuse his power like you did. In turn, I feel guilty that I harbor these doubts and suspicions.

"This mistrust and guilt has had a very real impact on both my physical and mental well-being. For example, when I started to realize what Larry had done to me, I avoided certain treatments that gymnasts rely upon, especially during intense Olympic training. I should have gotten massages three times a week or so, but I was too afraid (even if the therapist was a women). I lost confidence in my recovery, and this uncertainty began to undermine my training. Even today, I find myself scared that something bad will happen to me when I seek any medical treatment.

"The stress of training to make an Olympic team and competing in the games is all-consuming, and success demands laser focus. As my training ramped up, my stress about the competition increased. But added to that was the stress that came with trying to come to terms with the abuse, and constantly wondering how such a thing ever could have happened. This added layer of stress was more than I could handle. It was as though I couldn't begin to let myself believe what had happened to me. It was too much to bear.

"I have come to realize that everyone deals with trauma differently. As a gymnast, we are training to control our emotions under pressure. We become good at compartmentalizing. I became almost numb to my feelings. It was the only way I could survive the Olympic process. It was exhausting. The stress of constantly keeping certain thoughts in the back of my mind may have allowed me to focus in the moment, but it became more and more painful over time, both physically and emotionally. I knew when I finally allowed myself to feel again, it would be one of the hardest things I ever had to do.

"I was right. When I allowed myself to start thinking about what Larry had done, I was overcome by anxiety. I felt like I couldn't breathe, like someone was pushing on my chest and my throat was closing up. I couldn't sleep well because I would have terrible nightmares. I never felt rested.

The anxiety got so intense that I needed to see a doctor – a female – who prescribed anxiety medication so that I could function, and sleeping medication to help resolve my extreme exhaustion. After adjusting the dosages of some of the medication, I had a bad reaction and lost consciousness. I woke up to my terrified mom calling 911. I was loaded into an ambulance and taken to the hospital, where the doctors realized the issue was a side effect from one of the medications. My doctor has recommended that I try other medications to help me cope, but the trauma of what happened with those medications put me over the edge. It just added to the list of things I was anxious and stressed about.

"After this experience, I decided I needed to allow myself to feel what I had been suppressing for so long. I had spent so much time and energy trying to block out all the pain and trauma, and I realized it was just too much for me to contain. It was the most difficult period in my life. I was exhausted, barely able to do things I loved. I had no energy. I felt sad, anxious, and confused. I couldn't understand how someone could be so evil. And, painfully, Larry and his actions made me hate gymnastics for a time. Larry, you made me feel so uncomfortable and sad, and you made me believe the sport had let me down.

"I am trying now to take back my control, to remind myself that Larry has no power over me. It is never easy, but I am fighting to believe that the sport – which I do love – is independent of Larry and those who allowed him to do what he did. I've decided that I can't let him take gymnastics AWAY FROM ME.

"Despite my best efforts to regain control, I still have my triggers. My work requires frequent travel, and I feel anxious about traveling by myself. I find myself constantly looking around, paranoid and afraid to be alone. When I am at a hotel by myself and I order room service, I worry a male will deliver the food. I've had to develop strategies and coping mechanism. If a male knocks on the door, my heart begins to race. I hold the door open as he drops off the food and keep it open until he leaves. I often wonder if I am hurting their feelings by being so obviously distrusting of them. I always used to give people the benefit of the doubt, but if a decorated doctor who served on the national team for over thirty years turned out to be a monster, then how can I trust anybody? Now, I'll often catch myself being scared that people I meet are like Larry. And I hate that. I hate that Larry took away my trust of others.

"One of my best friends is also a victim of Larry – or a survivor, as I prefer to say. I thought we could be friends forever because we had gone through the best and worst moments together. But I think I remind her too much of what Larry did to us, and our friendship has suffered. Abuse isn't something you can just bring up with anyone, and I often wonder if I will ever find anyone like her, who gets me so well and knows just what to say to make me feel better.

"This situation has also affected my relationship with my parents, with whom I've always been extremely close. Over the past year, so many of my conversations with my parents have been about dealing with the trauma of what happened. I'm so grateful for their love and support, and I know I wouldn't be able to get through this without them, but I don't want to talk about him all the time.

"Still there are so many moving parts to figuring out how to process and understand the abuse. While training, I was often away from my family. Now that I finally have a more flexible schedule, I try to make up for lost time with my parents and siblings. I hate that Larry's abuse has affected my relationship with my family and how we interact. My sisters are in high school; one of them is in her senior year, a very exciting time. A lot of this past year has been about Larry, processing and dealing with his abuse, I try to discuss it with my parents when my sisters aren't around, but sometimes they walk into a room when we are talking about it and I can't help but feel bad that they have to worry about this. It is not fair. Abuse impacts the whole family.

"I want more than anything to make sure the next generation never goes through something like this. I don't want anyone to experience the pain, anxiety, fear, and other horrible feelings that stem from abuse. Every ninety-eight seconds another person experiences sexual assault, and sexual violence affects hundreds of thousands of Americans each year. That is hundreds of thousands too many. One in four girls and one in six boys will be molested before they turn eighteen. Too many abusers are master manipulators, who somehow make those they abuse feel guilty. And many find a way to convince adults to support and protect them.

"Larry's abuse started thirty years ago. At least that is the first reported incident. In those thirty years, many survivors came forward about Larry's abuse. Adult after adult, many in positions of authority, protected this monster, telling each survivor it was O.K., that Larry as not abusing them. Larry was decorated by USA Gymnastics, by the United States Olympic Committee – he was even named to an advisory board to come up with policies that would protect athletes from this kind of abuse!

"Knowing this is like being violated all over again. How many hundreds would have been saved if even one adult has listened and acted? It sickens me to know that for years and years, so many put an institution, or an organization, or medals, money, and reputation, above the safety and welfare of young, innocent people. We must listen and take proper action. Shame on all those who actively protected Larry and shame on those who looked the other way. Those who looked the other way are just as guilty. And shame on you, Larry, you are the worst example of humanity.

"Maybe by speaking out, by sharing my story and the way my daily life continues to be impacted by Larry's depraved actions, I can help other survivors feel less alone, less isolated, and encourage them to speak up and to get help.

"I ask that you give Larry the strongest possible sentence (which his actions deserve), for by doing so, you will send a message to him and to other abusers that they cannot get away with their horrible crimes; that they will be exposed for the evil they are, and they will be punished to the maximum extent of the law. Maybe knowing that Larry is being held accountable for his abuse will help me and the other survivors feel less alone, like we're being heard, and open up pathways for healing.

"I hope today you impose the maximum sentence the court allows, and I hope people begin to talk about how common and insidious abuse is. Every person we hold accountable for abuse makes a difference. Thank you."

CHAPTER TWENTY-SIX

My Bill Cosby Dilemma

First, my concern is not whether Bill Cosby raped women or not. I don't believe he actually "raped" ALL of them, but he obviously did something sexual with them using inappropriate means. He's a man, let's face it, and he's a very rich man with power to influence people and situations. I'll tell you this, if he did have sex with one woman or all of them, it's no different than what any other man in his position would have done. Since this #MeToo movement began, there's been an influx of allegations and charges. Listed at the very top of that heap is #45! I'm just saying…

Men are polygamists by nature. Their very anatomies allow them to be that way. That male appendage hanging between their legs is designed to enter any hole they so desire whenever their phallic symbol says, "Let's do it." Not only did my mama and daddy teach me that, but I learned it on my own. If you haven't learned it yet, you will if you deal with a man long enough.

But my dilemma is this…why did "they" wait so long to confront him with the issue? I mean, when I attended my first Bill Cosby comedy act at Western Michigan University in Kalamazoo, Michigan, around 1968-69, I was only fourteen years old and fell in love with his comedic style. And, yes, he joked about giving women the "Spanish Fly" drug to seduce them, but that was the "IN" thing to do and talk about at the time. I'd heard about Spanish Fly as an elementary student, so the concept had been floating around for quite some time.

It was the eve of the explosive sexual revolution and free love was the norm. EVERYBODY was doing "it," including "the judge." ("Here comes the judge, here come the judge.") That's when I also first heard talk of orgies, *ménage à trois*, and various other sexual activities. It's a sexually expressive baby-boomer thing.

The television show *Laugh-In* was gaining popularity, and we laughed when Goldie Hawn kept saying, "SOCK IT TO ME, SOCK IT TO ME!" That term spread like wildfire, as there were posters and T-shirts donning the suggestive phrase. I recall wearing my "SOCK IT TO ME" T-shirt when my appalled mother ordered me to "Take it off right now!" She thought it "shameful" that a young lady of my caliber would walk around advertising such a vile suggestion.

As an indicator of the times, I was equally shocked to learn that mama was such a fuddy-duddy. So not only did I take the T-shirt off, but watched as she cut it up and threw it in the trash. Yep. Those were the times that EVERYTHING had sexual innuendo AND follow through!

The songs like "It's Your Thing" by the Isley Brothers, and "Hot Stuff" by Donna Summer were hits on all charts. Young couples necked and petted when Marvin Gaye sang "Let's Get It On." People were dancing the "Freak" all over the nation and each other. It was a sign of the times.

Nobody took offense to Cosby's comedic approach, which was not only acceptable but encouraged by record sales. His album *It's Time, It's Time* reached #21 on the R&B Chart, and #37 on Billboard. He recorded the album before a live capacity-filled audience at Harrah's in Lake Tahoe, Nevada, and was even allotted extra time because of a musician's strike. Obviously, SOMEBODY was not only liking it, but endorsing and condoning it.

So what happened??! I'll tell you what happened. Bill Cosby got too big for his britches, and the powers that be, that one percent, the white male supremacists that we're learning have control of EVERYTHING in AmeriKKKa, including the Electoral College, had to stop him. Why? That Negro had the NERVE to consider buying NBC Television Network in 1992, and to add insult to injury, he tried to awaken black consciousness with his profound statements about the black family.

How dare you, Negro! "Your name is Toby, not Kunte Kinte," and we'll cut off your foot to show you! So they sent the great Negro Dr. William H.

Cosby BACK to the plantation where NEGROES like him belong. Essentially, THAT IS WHAT HAPPENED!

"They" let that Negro make all the money he wanted, and even allowed him to let little white kids climb all over him in Jell-O commercials with love and adoration. He became AmeriKKKa's DAD! Imagine that! A dark-skinned Negro was so loved by everyone that HE became the father figure of the nation!!

They even allowed him to receive the 2011 Presidential Award from the Advertising Hall of Fame, where he was cited as "one of the first Blacks to appear in the U.S. as an advertising person, AND the longest serving celebrity of a product line!"

Dr. William H. Cosby has been the advertising spokesperson for White Owl Cigars, Texas Instruments, E.F. Hutton, Kodak, and the 1990 Census. Imagine that…! The wealth he has acquired has him listed among the "top seven wealthiest Black philanthropists" in the country! The *Boston Globe* acknowledged Cosby as "one of the most cherished comedians in television history."

His television career spans nearly four decades! It is Bill Cosby who introduced us to the possibility of a "traditional Black family" where both parents were college-educated professionals (i.e. a doctor and lawyer). Many say it laid the groundwork/model for the election of the first black President of the United States in the person of Barack Obama, and his lovely wife, Michelle. But please know that white supremacists REALLY allowed that election to happen, so they could lull our senses for the whammy in the person of #45!

Let's look at the breadth, depth, and impact of his television shows/movie runs:

- *I Spy* with co-star Robert Culp – 1965–68 – 82 episodes

- *Fat Albert* cartoon show – 1972–1985 (13 years)

- *Uptown Saturday Night* movie – 1974

- *Let's Do It Again* movie – 1975

- Jell-O spokesperson – 1975–1991 (16 years)

- *A Piece of the Action* movie – 1977

- *The Cosby Show* – 1984–1992 (8 years)

- *A Different World* – 1987–1993 (6 years)

- *Little Bill* – 1999–2004 (5 years)

But, on January 10, 1997, a devastating tragedy rocked Bill and Camille Cosby's world. Their only son Ennis, age twenty-nine, was murdered in a so-called highway robbery in 1997 when his Mercedes Benz was disabled from a flat tire. According to a YouTube report from the late Dick Gregory, the Benz had a feature that enabled the car to still be drivable even with a flat tire. His Rolex watch and money were not disturbed in this robbery, however, tune in to Dr. Gregory's YouTube commentaries on that. The Nickelodeon television show *Little Bill* was produced in memory of Ennis.

But things started going awry with Mr. Cosby around 2004 when he appeared at a Rainbow Push national meeting as the guest of Reverend Jesse Jackson. I was there, proud to once again bask in my hero's presence, thirty-six years later, waiting with bated breath to hear what he had to say.

His words sounded judgmental, punitive, and cutting, but true. I'd never imagined Bill Cosby speaking in such a way. Not AmeriKKKa's dad! He sounded disgusted as he reamed our young black men for sagging pants, and then chided African American families for their "lack of parenting, poor academic performance, sexual promiscuity, and criminal behavior among the 'knuckleheads" of our community.

But the audience laughed and applauded. Nobody hissed or booed. Although, we as a people generally show more respect than that, still…! What's up with that? White male supremacists decided then that he had to be stopped!

Critics call it the "cultural divide" within the black community, which may be the case. But the truth hurts sometimes. I believe the powers that be didn't like his message to black AmeriKKKa because they might just listen, "turn from their wicked ways," as the Bible says, and God could "heal their land." While young black folks were angrily rejecting his message, the community as a whole stopped and said, "Hmmmmmm," he might have something there.

No! As long as society can blame its social ills on our black youth, they serve as the smokescreen for what is really happening in this country which is a covert and eternal crusade to protect white supremacy. Black youth cannot redeem themselves, since the black family has been decimated for 400 hundred years! Otherwise, the so-called Willie Lynch syndrome was all for naught. For more information about this, read, *Is Bill Cosby Right?* by Michael Eric Dyson. He's given too much to black college endowments and scholarships for African American students to be thrown to the wolves, and I don't believe that was his intent.

Should our anger for his brutal honesty cause us to turn our backs on him? Or did he strike a chord of reality in his assertion, albeit lacking in diplomacy? Did Dr. Cosby deserve a prison sentence while all other perpetrators went free? I think not.

"Four years ago, up and coming comedian Hannibal Buress took a crack at Bill Crosby that helped place him under scrutiny in Cosby's Philadelphia hometown. The joke would, as it turns out, have a dramatic effect and help draw attention to the claims levelled at Cosby by up to sixty women, many of whom had come forward with accusations against a powerful man in entertainment, only to largely be ignored." You don't think the "powers" already knew about his sexual proclivities? Think again…

"Pull your pants up, black people. I was on TV in the '80s," Buress, a black man said during the bit, referring to Cosby's time as the lead actor in *The Cosby Show*, and to Cosby's regular habit of telling black youth in America that 'the reason they lacked opportunity is because they were not behaving appropriately.'"

"Yeah, but you rape women, Bill Cosby," the joke continued… "So, turn the crazy down a couple notches." He then turned to members of the audience who may not have believed him, and said, "Check it out for yourselves. Google 'Bill Cosby rape…that…has more results than Hannibal Buress." (*The Independent*, Clark Mindock, NY 4/26/18)

"Days later, a short clip of the joke spread across the internet, bringing with it the attention of the national media, which was then watching the Cosby story intently as dozens of women came forward with their stories of Cosby assaulting them sexually." It's not because this was an unknown variable, but Cosby's time had come. That's why "they" jumped on it with a quickness. Besides, he would prove to be the perfect sacrificial lamb while all the guilty white men scattered.

"Some of the accusations had been publicly known previously, but the sheer number of women accusing the comedian of assault saw for Cosby a swift plunge in reputation…"

He was convicted of three criminal charges and faces up to thirty years in prison for the attacks. The statute of limitations has expired in many of the cases.

On April 26, 2018, at 6:11 p.m. the railroad tracks ended for actor/comedian/philanthropist Bill Cosby, as a Norristown, Pennsylvania, jury rendered a verdict of "guilty on all counts" of felony indecent aggravated assault, which carries a ten-year prison sentence for all three counts. That equals thirty years at maximum.

According to a *CBS News* account, he "was convicted of drugging and molesting a woman in the first big celebrity trial of the #MeToo era, completing the spectacular late-life downfall of a comedian who broke racial barriers in Hollywood on his way to television superstardom as America's dad." It said, "Cosby, 80, could end up spending his final years in prison…"

As I pen these closing chapters of my personal journey with sexual assault, I do so with great ambivalence, because while the movement is long overdue, I do believe justice has not been meted appropriately to perpetrators across racial lines. Yes, I believe Bill Cosby is being scapegoated, and no amount of talking with convince me otherwise.

Don't believe for one minute that they didn't know about these allegations years ago when Cosby first started hinting in his comedic skits about drugging women into sexual encounters, but they let that pass because EVERYBODY was doing it, all the big-time powerful men. Are you watching them fall right now? As Oprah Winfrey so deftly stated at the 2018 Oscar Awards, "Their Time is UP!!!"

But what about the women's accounts after so many years? I can't say anything about that, because I've waited forty years to share my own stories that have remained active in my psyche. I empathize with the victims, on one hand. I know all too well how it can gnaw at your peace of mind and self-esteem

My personal experience with sexual assault has been the vivid memory and shame that not only kept me quiet, but pierced my heart upon first learning of the #MeToo movement. I grimaced when hearing the testimony of senior statesman Congressman John Conyers (D-Michigan) had sexually assaulted one of his female assistants, because I, too, worked in the public sector for a high profile political figure. The empathy hit me hard and deep as I personalized her story more than any other.

It was at that pivotal point that I changed my mind about the next book I initially planned to write, and with a heavily convicted spirit I felt compelled to tell my story with a spirit heavily convicted while mourning the loss of one of AmeriKKKa's most prolific, effective, highly revered civil-rights advocates and high-ranking U.S. Congressman. John Conyers ascended the ranks and became one of the nation's premier statesmen. He knew and played the political game with deftness amidst tumultuous obstacles during his thirty-year tenure. But in the end, all for naught, as the wrong head led the way. What a profound disappointment.

Comedian/actor Eddie Griffin shared a plausible observation of the Cosby debacle with these words: "Eradication of legacy." He believes "great efforts are being expended to discredit the black man and continue the age-old practice of erasing his history, especially in the financial sense."

"Blacks do not leave this business clean," Griffin said. "Dr. Cosby, who deserves to be identified by his rightful moniker, is a class act. He mentored me and numerous comedians and actors by teaching us the game with encouragement to learn the business. He knew it was cut-throat. "

Griffin added, "you must keep in mind that these alleged

assaults took place in the seventies" when free love flowed, and inhibitions were cast aside. "Everybody was having sex with everybody else. Coke spoons were around everyone's neck, and everybody was going up to the hotel room with no shame or second thoughts. Who goes to a hotel room with a married man and don't expect to have sex?! But thirty years later, they call it rape! That's like I got robbed and call the police thirty years later to say, 'I got robbed!'

"There is a systematic effort to destroy every black male entertainer's image. They want all of us to have an asterisk by our names. Like Michael (Jackson) and Bill (Cosby), most African American male entertainers are singled out for their illicit behaviors. Nobody leaves this business clean. You're not going to die clean either.

"His decades of work are under attack," Griffin said. "The man systematically sent thousands of young brothers and sisters to college. He was so generous that he bought colleges for colleges. They're not messing with Roman Polanski though are they? What about him? He fled the country, but Cosby couldn't do that."

Minister Farrakhan said, "It took thirty years for a woman's nervous system to process where Cosby's hand was?!" He added, "Cosby is a good man who paid his dues. We all are evolving. Yes, he chided the black community for a dysfunctional lifestyle, but he was trying to teach another way of living a functional life. He was speaking TO us, not AT us and we took it out of context."

Dr. Cosby has now come full circle. The man who "was an example to AmeriKKKa, is now being used to set an example for sexual perpetrators everywhere." I am both saddened and troubled. Will this denigration of the black man EVER END? Will the threat and insecurity of the white male EVER be satisfied? Must he destroy the entire world to be made whole? Is penis envy THAT DEEP?

And on Tuesday, September 25, 2018, Dr. William H. Cosby, 81, was the first celebrity sentenced in the #MeToo era. According to National Public Radio, "the sentence completes the comedian's fall from groundbreaking cultural icon to convicted sex offender." He was found guilty for sexual assault and will spend at least three years in the Pennsylvania State Prison identified as number NN7687.

The Montgomery County judge who sentenced him with three to ten years said, "the words of Cosby's main accuser Andrea Constand citing that the entertainer took her 'beautiful, young spirit and crushed it' helped him reach his decision."

"In 2005, Constand, who was 32 years old at the time, reported to police in her native Ontario that Cosby had given her three blue pills and fondled her while she was incapacitated. Canadian police referred the case to authorities in Montgomery County, PA. The district Attorney Bruce Castor declined to press charges. Constand then pursued a civil lawsuit against the entertainer that was settled for $3.4 million.

"Fast forward to 2015 and at the request of the Associated Press, U.S. District Judge Eduardo Robreno, unsealed deposition testimony Cosby gave during that civil case in which he described obtaining Quaaludes to give women before sex. That revelation set off scores of other women to step forward and say Cosby drugged and molested or sexually assaulted them.

"The document also renewed interest in the District Attorney's Office to re-examine Constand's criminal case.

"Days before the statute of limitations was set to expire in December 2015, prosecutors summoned reporters to Montgomery County to make a startling announcement: Cosby was being charged with three counts of aggravated indecent assault over a more than decade-old incident.

"In the 2.5 years that followed, Cosby's case went to trial twice in Norristown, PA, not far from his estate where Constand says Cosby assaulted her. The first jury deadlocked in 2017 and a jury in the second trial convicted Cosby on all counts on April 26, 2018.

"Both times, Constand testified that during a visit to his house in 2004, Cosby gave her pills she believed were herbal supplements to help with stress she was having as she was considering a career change. When she took the pills, she became unconscious. She told jurors that while on a couch in his home and in a haze, she felt Cosby penetrating her with his fingers and using her hand to masturbate, as she was unable to fight back. 'I was frozen,' she told the jury.

"After six days of deliberation in 2017, jurors failed to reach a unanimous verdict resulting in a mistrial. Prosecutors did not give up, though, deciding to put Cosby on trial a second time. In April 2018, Cosby faced a different jury and in many ways, a whole new world.

"For one, the #MeToo movement had been unleashed, topping bad behaving men whose abuse had previously been kept secret. And the judge allowed five women in addition to Constand to take the stand and confront the famous comedian to help illustrate Cosby's pattern of predatory behavior. That was four more women than the judge permitted during the first trial. Legal experts say those women helped bolster the credibility of Constand.

"When the women took the witness stand, a pattern emerged. The women told the court that Cosby sought them out and gained their trust before arranging for private meetings, often under the guise of career advice or script coaching, at which Cosby would drug them, then sexually prey on them.

"Among the five women who took the stand in the second trial was model Janice Dickinson, who, along with the other accuser witnesses, Cosby's lawyers attempted to paint as a fame-seeking liar who had fabricated stories to smear a famous person.

They also challenged accuser Janice Baker-Kinney's delayed accusation.

"You said words to the effect that, 'For 30 years, I didn't know I had been raped,' said Cosby attorney Thomas Mesereau during cross-examination. 'So, for 30 years you didn't think anyone had sexually assaulted you?'

"It still takes me everything within my being to say the words 'I was raped,' because I still carry the guilt," responded Baker-Kinney.

"Throughout the proceeding, Cosby's legal team maintained the comedian's innocence, arguing that the encounter with Constand was consensual. In the first trial, Cosby's lawyers emphasized an alleged mutual romance between Cosby and Constand. With the retooled legal team for the second trial, Cosby's lawyers had a new approach: attempting to portray Constand as a 'con artist' who had long planned to concoct false allegation against Cosby in order to secure a multi-million-dollar payout." (National Public Radio NPR/Laura Benshoff and Bobby Allyn/9/25/18)

In hearing the court proceedings, admittedly I am deeply saddened to learn that my hero is a sexual predator just as my father, his father's stepson, my deceased pastor, a civil-rights leader, and two male supervisors were. I've walked in those shoes and tried to endure the pain, guilt, and shame associated with such a travesty.

But I still believe Bill Cosby is being scapegoated here and I'm anxious to see what happens to so many high-profile, white male perpetrators. I believe Judge Steven O'Neill derived pleasure in sentencing the wealthy philanthropist who won awards for being the premier African American on the advertising front!

"It's time for justice, Mr. Cosby," said Judge Steven O'Neill. "This has all circled back to you."

This punishment of the first celebrity prison sentence of the #MeToo movement is on the "higher end of Pennsylvania's guidelines for someone who has been convicted of aggravated indecent assault." Dr. Cosby's lawyers argued for more than two days that he "should be placed on house arrest" due to his age, health conditions, and no prior convictions. Requests that the actor be released on bail as defense begins the appeals process were denied. Bill Cosby was ordered into custody immediately following sentencing.

"Cosby took off his jacket and rolled up his sleeves and could be seen laughing with his legal team before sheriff's deputies handcuffed him and escorted him out of the courtroom. As he shuffled by a sea of reporters, the comedian's thin wooden cane was between his handcuffed wrists…"

Prosecutors asked the court to require Cosby to cover the cost of two trials, which added up to about $420,000.

CHAPTER TWENTY-SEVEN

White Male Fragility

The U.S. Senate Judiciary Committee's Democratic members are urging President Trump to "withdraw his nomination of Brett Kavanaugh to the Supreme Court or order an FBI investigation in the multiple sexual misconduct charges against the judge.

"Three women, Christine Blasey Ford, Deborah Ramirez and Julie Swetnick, have accused Kavanaugh of sexual misconduct." They believe "Judge Kavanaugh is being considered for a promotion" via the nomination.

"The standard of character and fitness for a position on the nation's highest court must be higher than this," their written statement read. "Judge Kavanaugh has staunchly declared his respect for women and issued blanket denials of any possible misconduct, but those declarations are in serious doubt."

Senate Majority Leader Chuck Schumer (D-NY) called on Kavanaugh to "withdraw from consideration following the release of the allegations" and urged Senate Republicans to 'immediately suspend' confirmation proceedings due to 'multiple, corroborated allegations' against him."

Senator Cory Booker (D-NJ), who also belongs to the Senate Judiciary Committee, concurred with Schumer's recommendation.

"Christine Blasey alleges Kavanaugh pinned her down, groped her and attempted to remove her clothes during a small party when they were both high school students.

"A week later, the *New Yorker* reported accusations from Deborah Ramirez, who alleges Kavanaugh thrust his penis in her face during a drinking party when they were both freshmen at Yale University in the early 1980s.

Julie Swetnick "alleges she witnessed Kavanaugh and one of his friends at several high school parties (in the 1980s) getting 'drunk' and 'being overly aggressive with girls.' "She claims to be "the victim of a 'gang rape' and Kavanaugh was present."

As I watched the televised proceedings and marveled at Kavanaugh's rage and tears versus Blasey-Ford's composure, I felt pity for the predator who'd finally been caught for an unreported crime he committed more than thirty-five years ago. Yes, it has damaged his family and reputation, but what about Blasey-Ford? Has she not suffered from his reckless behavior that has haunted her just as long?

How long must women carry the baggage of misogynists who believe a woman's purpose is to appease their three-minute sexual efforts? She didn't have the luxury of expressing or demonstrating anger or tears to avoid the stereotypical perception of emotionalism steeped in gender bias and stereotype.

As Senator Majority Leader Chuck Schumer (D-NY) calls for Brett Kavanaugh to withdraw from the U.S. Supreme Court candidacy, President Donald Trump said this in a tweet, "Avenatti (attorney for the three women) is a third-rate lawyer who is good at making false accusations, like he did on me and like he is now doing on Judge Brett Kavanaugh. He is just looking for attention and doesn't want people to look at his past record and relationships – a total low-life!" (*HuffPost* by Hayley Miller 9/26/18).

And in the final hours of a decision pro or con for Kavanaugh, Senator Susan Colllins (R-Maine) says she will vote "yes" on behalf of Kavanaugh's confirmation. This shocking decision led in the Maine People's Alliance and Mainers for Accountable Leadership "begging Senator Collins to vote 'no.'" They indicated that "if you fail to stand up for the people of Maine and for American's across the country, EVERY dollar donated to this campaign will go to your eventual Democratic opponent in 2020. WE WILL GET YOU OUT OF OFFICE!"

At the time of Brett Kavanaugh's confirmation to the U.S. Supreme Court, approximately three million dollars of a multi-million-dollar campaign has been raised nationwide to oust her.

On October 18, 2018, the *Huffington Post* reported "with Brett Kavanaugh's confirmation, the Republicans have secured their place as essentially the last bastion of male dominance in a Me Too world!"

CHAPTER TWENTY-EIGHT

The Final Analysis

Who would have imagined that with the election of a national leader who glamorizes and makes statements like "grabbing women by their GENITALS," would remain in the highest office of the land with no repercussions, thereby condoning misogyny against women!?

And who would have imagined that not only would this issue come to light, finally emancipating women's minds, bodies, and spirits to release and let go of these vile, sexual acts of violence that deeply mar the beautiful act of sexuality that God created for man and woman to enjoy together?

These behaviors span the professional ranks, leaving no man in any position of power or otherwise to hide behind cloaks of deceit and male dominance any longer. As Oprah Winfrey so eloquently and victoriously stated, "THEIR TIME really IS UP!" It is because of divine providence that this has happened at this moment in time.

I certainly do not believe male dominance is what God meant when he initially created man, nor when he made us as man's help-meet (Genesis 2:21). Nor was white-male privilege God's intention when "He made man in his own image" (Genesis 1:27) or "created woman out of the rib of man" (Genesis 2:23). God said in Genesis 3:15, "…I will put enmity between thee (man) and woman, and between thy seed and her seed; it shall bruise thy heel."

Finally, in Genesis 3:16, God decided that woman's "desire shall be to thy husband and he shall rule over thee." Men have taken these few statements literally. It's destroying relationships, families, perceptions, and self-esteem. Most importantly, it has destroyed WOMEN!

Many men, Christian or otherwise, take these few passages without reading the whole verse or having no understanding of the Spirit of God. It is because of this that men feel entitled to denigrate, manipulate, and victimize women as the weaker sex. NOT SO. As evidenced by the year 2018, God is doing a totally new thing through women and the best is yet to come. I say this in all humility because I know that HE is sovereign and has the final word. It's no coincidence that the denigration of women has come to light. OUR TIME HAS COME!

That's not meant as a "feminist rant." I've heard reference to feminism as male emasculation or belittlement. Again, NOT SO, and our strong, confident, self-actualized men know this. Hopefully, they can enlighten the lesser men who have the pitiful need to dominate women to feel powerful and almighty.

On another note to my Black men, although I feel sadness and sorrow for Dr. Cosby, I am reminded how brothers flock to white women when they feel defeated or reach their pinnacle of success, as if she is their trophy prize, that beacon of light that will see them through. This goes back to the days when she was flaunted as forbidden fruit and, like Eve in the Garden of Eden, you LOVE TO EAT THEREOF! You have HISTORICALLY abandoned your Black queen for that white woman who invariably cries "RAPE" whenever she doesn't have her way or the upper hand, and you continue to pay for PICKING FROM THE WRONG TREE! That holds true even today, in 2018!!! WILL YOU EVER LEARN, NEGRO?

Do you think you are any different than our own Emmett Till, who, at the innocent age of a mere fourteen years old, allegedly whistled at a white woman and was brutally murdered beyond recognition because that lily-white princess said HE did it, only to learn fifty years later that it was all a lie?

Did not the white woman, albeit a lesbian, and a slew of other white females cry rape on Bill Cosby? Look at him now, sentenced to three years in a standard six-by-eight-foot jail cell that some "knucklehead" occupied before him, and with all the money, power, and influence that he can muster, he WILL NOT BE ALLOWED TO PASS GO! Dr. Cosby's actions and words have relegated his rich black butt BACK TO THE PLANTATION! White supremacy has reminded Dr. Cosby of who he is in their eyes. "TOBY!"

When will you learn, black man, that WE are your mainstay? That the white man has been destroying our families and relationships for generations, maintaining with great confidence that the "divide and conquer" philosophy rings true to this day? And the white woman is the ultimate prize that will ultimately SUCK THE VERY LIFE FROM YOU…

Yes, black-on-black relationships have their issues, but why do you keep taking the easy way out by flocking to white women who know nothing of our shared experience? If you continue this path, you are selling out and we both know it. You don't have a problem in laying that black pipe and stroking that silky hair that a-DICKS the white female and reinforces fear and penis envy in their men, fueling their fears.

Of course, this doesn't pertain to all white women, as there are some who develop and maintain strong, black families, but until they learn how to COMB THAT BABY'S HAIR, chances are great that they will continue to fall short. A shared experience, upbringing, culture, and family structure is essential for strong families and let's face it, you will ALWAYS be viewed as the NEGRO who might possibly get rejected when "coming to dinner" at their table! "GUESS WHO'S COMING TO DINNER, NEGRO?" Not you if you try to equate yourself with them. Ask Bill…

So, Dr. Cosby, you dogged black folks out while secretly sleeping white. You introduced the community to healthy black role models, lifestyle, and black art, had an all-black cast and black cartoon characters, BUT you harshly and openly criticized a dysfunctional black family structure that was designed by a racist system, all the while "putting family business in the streets." I'm so upset with you, I don't know what to do!

And Larry Nassar! While I was sitting up there enjoying women's gymnastics and prize-winning Olympic competitions, you were ABUSING those little girls?! Feeling all between their little legs, grabbing their genitals, and watching child pornography?! Those babies were thriving under THOSE CONDITIONS, too! SHAME ON YOU! It's a painful reminder for me of a childhood fraught with confusion, fear, and shame as my own sick daddy was fondling my breasts every chance he got, causing me to walk around the house with my arms folded. And, YOU, Dr. Nassar, had the nerve to lie about it all. Thank God for the birth of this movement, or your shady practices wouldn't have been exposed. #METOO!

Then there are the other clowns…Weinstein, Monrove, Kavanaugh, Sheen, Conyers…REALLY?! Your façade of being so stellar and high-ranking has finally crumbled because you, too, were abusing/assaulting women all along!? DISGUSTING.

Let's not forget about my father, my dead pastor, my former bosses, my dad's stepbrother, the deceased Michigan Legislator, the deceased NAACP national leader, the prominent Detroit minister/civil-rights leader who STILL positions himself front-row center as if he's THE BIG MAN! All y'all can burn in HELL as far as I'm concerned because just as you did it to me, you've done it to others, causing irreparable psychological damage that we keep trying to stuff to stay focused, survive, and feel good about ourselves!

It's been a long, painful journey, but I believe the nightmare is about to end socially. Now we must begin to heal emotionally/psychologically. That's the hard part.

It is my solemn prayer that EVERY victim of sexual assault in any form will share her own story in some small way. Whether it is talking to a professional or merely writing about your experience in a personal journal. The importance is in getting it out of your mind and heart. It doesn't matter how long you've been holding the assault or how deeply you've stored it. The key is to release it into the atmosphere because it's too toxic to carry. Our bodies and minds cannot thrive with the poisons. Trust me. I know.

I stated in the beginning that "I was groomed for sexual assault." That's based on family dysfunction and life experience, BUT I was created by God to be equal, free, and whole. And you were too!

~ END ~

www.ingramcontent.com/pod-product-compliance
Lightning Source LLC
Chambersburg PA
CBHW070658100726
47907CB00007B/2260